Bolan had no time to search for the preacher, rescue him a second time, then double back to meet with Grimaldi. He'd have to scrub the airlift yet again. He wasn't sure if Abner rated any further effort, but that wasn't Bolan's call. He still felt duty-bound to try at least once more. And after that?

Hell, you could only save a man so many times if he was bent on suicide. Beyond a certain point, it was both futile and ridiculous.

The trail was easy to follow, Braga's people making no attempt to hide their tracks. They had their prize and would be hurrying back home to show it off.

Unless the Executioner could stop them first.

MACK BOLAN ®

The Executioner

The Executioner®
Don Pendleton's
AMAZON IMPUNITY

A GOLD EAGLE BOOK FROM
WORLDWIDE®

TORONTO • NEW YORK • LONDON
AMSTERDAM • PARIS • SYDNEY • HAMBURG
STOCKHOLM • ATHENS • TOKYO • MILAN
MADRID • WARSAW • BUDAPEST • AUCKLAND

In Memoriam Glen Doherty, Sean Smith,
Christopher Stevens, Tyrone Woods Benghazi,
Libya: Sept. 11, 2012

Recycling programs
for this product may
not exist in your area.

First edition March 2014

ISBN-13: 978-0-373-64424-7

Special thanks and acknowledgment to
Mike Newton for his contribution to this work.

AMAZON IMPUNITY

Printed in U.S.A.

RETRIBUTION, n. A rain of fire-and-brimstone that falls alike upon the just and such of the unjust as have not procured shelter by evicting them.

—Ambrose Bierce,
The Devil's Dictionary

Retribution is my business, not revenge. The predators I hunt have made themselves fair game. I'm not their judge or jury; I'm their executioner.

—Mack Bolan

THE
MACK BOLAN
LEGEND

Nothing less than a war could have fashioned the destiny of the man called Mack Bolan. Bolan earned the Executioner title in the jungle hell of Vietnam.

But this soldier also wore another name—Sergeant Mercy. He was so tagged because of the compassion he showed to wounded comrades-in-arms and Vietnamese civilians.

Mack Bolan's second tour of duty ended prematurely when he was given emergency leave to return home and bury his family, victims of the Mob. Then he declared a one-man war against the Mafia.

He confronted the Families head-on from coast to coast, and soon a hope of victory began to appear. But Bolan had broken society's every rule. That same society started gunning for this elusive warrior—to no avail.

So Bolan was offered amnesty to work within the system against terrorism. This time, as an employee of Uncle Sam, Bolan became Colonel John Phoenix. With a command center at Stony Man Farm in Virginia, he and his new allies—Able Team and Phoenix Force—waged relentless war on a new adversary: the KGB.

But when his one true love, April Rose, died at the hands of the Soviet terror machine, Bolan severed all ties with Establishment authority.

Now, after a lengthy lone-wolf struggle and much soul-searching, the Executioner has agreed to enter an "arm's-length" alliance with his government once more, reserving the right to pursue personal missions in his Everlasting War.

Prologue

State of Mato Grosso, Brazil

"How much farther now?" Artur da Rochas asked.

"You'll know when we get there," Luiz Aranha said.

"Walking all this way because some wretched preacher wants to save the Indians is stupid."

"Why don't you go back and tell that to *o chefe?*" Aranha suggested.

"What? And get my head cut off for nothing? *Vai te fuder.*"

"Watch yourself," Aranha warned him. "You forget your place."

"My place is back at camp, with my Lucélia," said da Rochas, lightening the mood.

"Don't bet that she's waiting for you while you're gone."

"She loves me!"

"I've no doubt of that. And others, too."

"You're jealous," said da Rochas, but he sounded worried.

Someone else was grumbling now, back in the ranks. Over his shoulder, Aranha snapped, "Shut your mouth!" He was sick of the complaints each time they went out on patrol. What else had these idiots expected when they'd volunteered for duty in the Amazon? Some kind of luxury retreat?

No. Their job was tramping through the jungle on whatever mission was assigned to them. They dressed in sweaty camouflage fatigues, soaked through with rain no less than half a dozen times each day. They carried IMBEL MD-2 assault rifles, standard issue for the Brazilian army, chambered for 5.56 mm NATO rounds, plus a motley collection of handguns, hatchets, knives and other weapons of personal preference. All of them were hardened killers—some former military men—and still they whined like children when required to do a job.

That was the hitch with criminals, Luiz Aranha thought. No dedication. It was something that set him apart.

Or maybe not.

He didn't relish the patrols either, but he had sense enough to keep his mouth shut, knowing that dissension in the ranks was bound to irritate *o chefe* and produce some dire results. If nothing else, tight lips ensured some measure of immunity.

As for their targets, nothing on earth could help them now. They had provoked *o chefe*'s wrath, and they were bound to suffer for it. Aranha had been ordered to bring them back alive. Slogging through the jungle, watching out for snakes along the way, he wondered how they would die for his master's pleasure.

Whatever *o chefe* had in mind, it should be memorable. An example to his men and to outsiders who offended him.

A little bit of Hell on Earth.

Missão Misericórdia

MERCY MISSION—OR *Missão Misericórdia,* in the native Portuguese—was not found on any map of the Brazilian jungle. Truth be told, few souls beyond a radius of fifty miles were conscious of the small outpost's existence. It was not affiliated with a major church, received no stipend from a lavish headquarters in the United States or Europe, and had never aired a single plea for help on radio or television. It was not forgotten by the outside world, so much as overlooked entirely.

The mission was a two-person operation with a shoestring budget, driven by the conviction that each person on the planet had an equal right to hear the word of God and find salvation through His grace. Its placement in the Mato Grosso had resulted from a challenge offered and accepted in a suburb of Miami, Florida, two years before.

You want to save the heathens, someone had demanded, *you should try the Indians in South America. Not many of them are left, but it should satisfy your martyr complex.*

Abner Cronin didn't think he *had* a martyr complex, but he took the gibe to heart. He'd discussed it with his wife and had sympathized with her instinctive reservations, so they took it to the Lord and let Him settle the debate.

All systems were go—except for cash, supplies and anything resembling knowledge of the area.

They'd done their homework though and had picked a tribe—the Munduruku—that was verging on extinction after centuries of conflict with slavers, prospectors, rubber traders, loggers, petroleum wildcatters and the junta that had ruled Brazil from 1964 to 1985. Even today, incursions on the Mundurukus' homeland continued to decimate the wildlife and the rain forest itself, forcing the tribe closer to the forbidding border of Bolivia.

Abner Cronin and his wife, Mercy, had given up their reasonably comfortable lives to serve God's wretched and forgotten children in the wilderness. The mission was named in Mercy's honor, both a serendipitous coincidence and Abner's personal acknowledgment that Mercy's sacrifice in leaving Florida was greater than his own. She'd hoped for children there, something approxi-

mating a normal life, but had surrendered all her modest
dreams at his behest.

There were days—and many of them—when he thought
she must regret that choice, but Mercy Cronin never failed
to grace him with a smile, encourage him when he faltered
or welcome their parishioners, who must have seemed as
alien to her as any creature from a distant star. She'd dealt
with serpents and malarial mosquitoes, ticks and leeches,
spiders larger than a dinner plate, vampire bats and jaguars, not to mention all the forest's other creeping vermin.
They'd survived a brush with unfriendly villagers before
they had even reached their final destination and had lost
a pack mule to piranhas on the journey.

Am I a martyr yet? he wondered and almost smiled.

The usual contingent of Mundurukus had assembled for
his Sunday sermon, twenty-five in all. Three men, five ad-
olescent boys, the rest women and younger children. They
were learning English slowly, as the Cronins had begun
to learn the tribe's language and sufficient Portuguese to
bargain for supplies on monthly trips into Cáceres, on the
Rio Paraguai. Communication was a work in progress,
true enough, but they were making strides toward understanding. Moving closer every day to a successful meeting of the mind and soul.

His lesson for the day was drawn from John 3:16.

For God so loved the world, that he gave his only be-
gotten Son, that whosoever believeth in him should
not perish, but have everlasting life.

If they could only master that, the rest would fall naturally into place.

Abner had welcomed everyone and was launching the
discussion in his awkward, halting way, when Mercy suddenly appeared, a strained expression on her normally

intrepid face. He recognized the look of trouble and was about to ask what the problem was, when rifle shots rang out and some members of his congregation toppled from their rough-hewn wooden benches.

Abner bolted from the pulpit to confront a mob of ten to fifteen men, armed and wearing paramilitary garb. Their leader was a man he recognized and feared, but Abner stood before him, rigid, while screaming survivors fled into the forest, leaving the dead and wounded in their wake.

The raiding party's point man stopped within arm's reach. Mercy was at Abner's side now, lending strength as always.

"You were warned," the gunman said. "You did not listen."

"I have listened to my Lord," Abner replied—then buckled, as the leader slashed his rifle's butt into the missionary's stomach.

Whispering a breathless prayer, Abner could not help thinking, maybe I'm a martyr, after all.

1

State of Mato Grosso, Brazil

Viewed from an altitude of sixteen thousand feet, the tree-tops rushing past below resembled crowded garden shrubs. In reality the jungle giants loomed two hundred feet or more off the ground. A drop from that height was beyond extreme.

Which wouldn't stop Mack Bolan, aka the Executioner, from attempting it.

"Five minutes," said his pilot, Jack Grimaldi, speaking through his oxygen mask.

Wearing his own O2 mask and giving Grimaldi a thumbs-up from the Cessna 182T's open doorway, Bolan's gaze fixed on the treescape below. It felt as if he could step out, drop briefly, then stroll across the treetops, just an amble over a manicured lawn. A glance at his altimeter would shatter that illusion, just as Bolan's bones would shatter if he hit the forest canopy from the wrong angle.

The Cessna had been Grimaldi's first and only choice for HALO jumping over the Mato Grosso. Its cruising speed was 164.5 miles per hour, powered by a single Lycoming O-540 six-cylinder engine. Unlike most private aircraft, the Cessna's door opened upward—so it wouldn't flap and slam on the jumper.

HALO. *H*igh *A*ltitude, *L*ow *O*pening, also known as a

military free fall. Boiled down to basics, a HALO jumper hurls himself into space at altitudes ranging from fifteen- to thirty-five-thousand feet, deploying his parachute at the last feasible moment.

Bolan was dressed to drop, complete with a helmet and insulated jumpsuit, gloves and military free-fall boots, bailout oxygen and a Vigil 2 automatic activation device that would fire a small pyrotechnic charge to open his main chute when Bolan reached the target altitude of 2,800 feet above treetop level.

He was also dressed to kill, beginning with his choice of combat rifles: the ultrareliable, nearly indestructible Steyr AUG, chambered in 5.56 mm NATO, with a standard 1.5-power telescopic sight and a flash hider doubling as a launcher for rifle grenades. Bolan's backup weapons included a Desert Eagle Mark VII semiauto pistol chambered in .44 Magnum; a SIG Sauer P226 Tactical Operations semiauto chambered in 9 mm Parabellum, with its extended muzzle threaded to accommodate suppressors; a classic Mark I trench knife and an all-purpose bolo knife for clearing vegetation.

Anticipating hang-ups in the forest canopy, Bolan carried a knife to cut the lines, and he wore a pair of Bucklite titanium climbing spurs strapped to his boots. His belt supported two military-standard canteens, while his Warfighter three-day assault pack—worn on front, against his thighs on bailout, to accommodate the backup parachute riding on his chest, the primary one on his back—contained MREs, a mess kit, first-aid kit, a sat phone, night-vision goggles, a GPS tracker, a Maglite tactical flashlight and sundry other items.

Beneath the insulated jumpsuit, which Bolan would abandon after landing, he was clad in fatigues stitched from insect-repellent fabric patterned in universal camouflage. Bolan had streaked his face with camouflage paint, as well. A longtime veteran of jungle fighting, he could merge with any landscape as required, achieving near invisibility.

But first he had to make that drop and reach the ground.

"One minute, now," Grimaldi warned.

Bolan began to run the numbers. He was about to step out of an airplane and plummet through space at speeds approaching terminal velocity. After three-quarters of a minute in a free fall, his automatic activation device would deploy the main chute. If that failed, he still had the rip cord and a reserve chute strapped to his chest—assuming there was time to use it before he crashed into the treetops.

Terminal velocity, indeed, if anything went wrong.

Bolan would have to leap well clear of the Cessna to avoid a tail strike that would turn his free fall into a death drop. With his head down and arms against his sides, he'd be dropping like a bomb toward ground zero, then using his arms and legs to navigate until the main chute opened to decelerate his fall.

The chute itself was an AS33-Intruder model from AS Airborne Systems, which featured a nine-cell ram air canopy with antistall modifications to minimize injuries on touchdown.

Unless, of course, you planned on landing in a jungle canopy, hundreds of feet above the ground.

At that point, you were on your own.

"Time!" Grimaldi said.

Bolan shoved off and hurtled into howling space.

FORTY-FIVE SECONDS can feel like an hour in a free fall. Ferocious winds peel back the skydiver's lips and ripple his cheeks, whip at his limbs and body, driving him off course unless he's learned to navigate with arms and legs while plummeting toward impact. If the jumper isn't screaming, an impressive silence overcomes the world. It's possible to lose touch with reality, enter a state of self-hypnosis and forget to keep an eye on the altimeter or to pull the rip cord, which is where the Vigil 2 comes in. A *pop,* a jolt and suddenly the chute is open. Just as suddenly the jumper must display a whole new range of navigational skills.

All jungles are composed of layers. The looming giants are emergent trees that make up the upper canopy, their huge branches expanding above smaller neighbors. In Brazil, those giants are known as *angelim pedra*— "angel's heart." Next comes the main canopy, trees with broad crowns filling gaps between the giants, their limbs a home for orchids, bromeliads and lichens. Lower still is the shrub layer, consisting of young trees and smaller woody plants; and underneath is the field layer, with its seedlings, ferns and scattered herbs. Finally, in perpetual shade, the jungle floor is paved with fallen leaves and rotting vegetation.

Bolan's task was to avoid the thrusting crowns of the emergent giants and penetrate the lower canopy with minimal damage to himself or his equipment. After disengaging from his parachute harness, he'd descend to ground level and take up the hunt. His drop zone had been picked with GPS precision, supplemented by the latest aerial photographs. He knew exactly how the chosen stretch of jungle should appear to someone swooping from a bird's-eye view, and what he saw below him matched the photographs.

It almost worked.

No one could photograph the wind, however, or predict when it would suddenly lash out to spoil a puny human's best-laid plans. The gust that caught his chute drove Bolan east, a hundred yards or so off course. Not much, in terms of hiking distance—but he wasn't hiking. He was *falling,* and the tree beneath him now, soon to make impact, seemed to be the tallest angel's heart for half a mile around.

A last-second tug on Bolan's left-hand riser spared him from being impaled on a thrusting branch. Then he was *in* the tree and grappling with the chute's suspension lines as another gust caught the Intruder's canopy and whipped it westward, trying hard to take its passenger along for the ride. Bolan found the quick-release clasps on his harness, unsnapped them and sagged with relief as the chute sailed off without him.

He took a rapid inventory of his limbs and digits, found them all in working order and proceeded to adjust his gear. His small reserve chute was the first item to go, left slung over a branch where it would ultimately rot away or make a nest for birds. Bolan shifted his assault pack to his shoulders, adjusting its padded straps. He left the crash helmet and goggles on for safety's sake, in case he slipped somewhere along the way and came too close to jutting, eye-gouging twigs. The headgear also would protect his face and scalp from nervous tree-dwellers.

Because the canopy was alive.

Brightly colored birds and butterflies were the most obvious treetop inhabitants, but they were not alone. A teeming world of invertebrates, reptiles, amphibians and mammals lived among the upper reaches of the jungle, some never descending to the forest floor until they died and their bodies dropped to feed the scavengers below. Others would cling to their high perches even after death, until decomposition turned them into fertilizer for the other plants that strove for sunlight at the apex of the canopy.

Most tree-dwellers were harmless, but Bolan could still be swarmed by ants or wasps as he descended, bitten by a viper or a lethal Brazilian wandering spider. Even a nonvenomous boa, if startled, might sink its backward-slanting teeth into Bolan's face or neck, and throw its coils around him, toppling Bolan from his perch to certain doom.

So, easy does it on the long way down, trusting his

climbing spikes and strength to get him back on terra firma.

One step at a time, he started to descend.

MERCY CRONIN DID her best to hide the terror threatening to overwhelm her. She slogged and stumbled through the forest in her husband's footsteps, gunmen marching out in front and coming up behind them, pressing close. If she slowed down, the man behind her snarled and jabbed her with the muzzle of his automatic rifle, laughing when she yelped in pain. That mockery had prompted her into a stubborn silence, and she kept pace with the grim parade as best she could.

Why are we still alive? she wondered. It made no sense. Threats against their mission had increased during the past few months—had become almost routine—although the source was not identified. Abner had explained that several elements were bent on driving the Mundurukus and the other forest tribes from their ancestral homes and hunting grounds—loggers and oil men, cattle barons who would raze the rain forest and turn it into grazing land. A mission was an anchor for the aborigines, and education worked against the common propaganda line that they were hopeless savages.

The Cronins had endured the threats and prayed, trusting God to keep them and the Mundurukus safe. Now that the worst had happened—the murder of their innocent parishioners—and Abner and Mercy were witnesses, logic said she and her husband were living on borrowed time. Whoever had dispatched these goons to raid Missão Misericórdia surely could not allow eyewitnesses to live. The easy thing—the smart thing, from a murderer's perspective—would have been to kill Mercy and Abner outright, and bury them or let the jungle consume their flesh and bones.

So, once again, why are they still alive?

The question frightened Mercy, but the answers offered by her mind were even worse.

It couldn't be a kidnapping for ransom. She and Abner had no wealthy relatives or backers in the States—no church with deep pockets would bail them out of danger. On the contrary, they'd burned their bridges when they had left Miami for Brazil two years ago. The U.S. State Department might protest their abduction, but the Cronins were not prominent or wealthy—no one worthy of a rescue operation or any negotiation with a gang of terrorists. Perhaps they would secure fifteen minutes of fame in some media markets back home, but Mercy knew they would be forgotten just as quickly.

Why abduct them then?

Perhaps to make them an example, which had terrifying implications. Mercy pictured graphic scenes of torture and humiliation, their mutilated corpses left beside some forest road or even dropped off in Cáceres as a warning to any who might follow their lead in aiding the native tribes. The visions left her weak and trembling, wishing she could cling to Abner's hand, but her kidnappers had secured their wrists behind their backs with plastic ties.

That made hiking through the jungle doubly awkward, as they trudged through mud, tripped over roots or slipped on ridges thick with fallen, rotting leaves. When someone up ahead released a springy branch or dangling creeper, Mercy had to duck or let it slap her in the face, stinging her cheeks. She couldn't fan away the swarms of flying, biting insects but was forced to squint her eyes instead—which then obscured the narrow shaded trail and made her prone to stumbling. If she fell, her sole recourse was twisting to one side, taking the impact on her arm and shoulder, rather than her face.

All in all, it was a march of misery with cruel death waiting at its end.

Back in Miami, some of their acquaintances had taunted Abner, not quite joking when they'd claimed her husband sought a martyr's fate in the Brazilian wilderness. Mercy, who knew Abner's heart and shared his passion, thought those people were wrong. But now, it seemed, their gibes would be borne out. When word got back to Florida, their former friends would sit nodding over coffee or cocktails, saying that they'd known what to expect from the beginning. She and Abner would be branded fools, but even that was covered in the Good Book.

Apostle Paul had said to the Corinthians:

We are fools for Christ's sake, but ye are wise in Christ; we are weak, but ye are strong; ye are honorable, but we are despised.

And also had preached:

For after that in the wisdom of God the world by wisdom knew not God, it pleased God by the foolishness of preaching to save them that believe.

It troubled her that she couldn't draw comfort from the scriptures under the threat of agonizing death. Was her weakness proof that she didn't deserve salvation? Would she be forgotten by her Lord as well as the world at large?

Another jab into her back made Mercy stumble, almost falling, but she kept her balance, slogging on.

Toward Judgment Day.

IT TOOK BOLAN the better part of forty minutes to climb down the huge trunk of the angel's heart that had broken his fall. A sense of urgency was driving him, but one false move could mean a broken arm or leg, maybe a broken neck, and that would be the end of it.

The end of him.

So Bolan took his time, setting his spikes on one boot, then the other, using any handholds he could find along the downward path, from limbs to vines as thick as steamship mooring lines. The vines couldn't be used for the acrobatics of a Tarzan movie, since they clung to looming trunks with grim determination—some eventually strangling their hosts—but they served as a rope ladder of sorts for Bolan's descent.

A spider monkey watched him for a while, remaining carefully beyond arm's reach and studying its larger relative, clucking advice or criticism as the spirit moved it. Bolan wasn't worried about monkey bites—not from a single specimen, at least—but he stayed alert as he dropped lower, watching out for scorpions and tree vipers. A sting from the former likely wouldn't kill him, but viper venom produced fever, nausea with bloody vomiting, unconsciousness and death.

Bolan's first-aid kit included two syringes of antivenin, one to combat the neurotoxic venom common among coral snakes around the world—including at least four species found in Brazil—the other for the hemotoxic venom injected by most New World vipers.

Bolan scrambled down the vast tree trunk, sweating inside his insulated jumpsuit. On touchdown, he would shed the suit and bury it with his entrenching tool to avoid tipping off enemy patrols.

Would they be out in force? He couldn't say, but training and experience had taught him not to take unnecessary chances. Bolan's targets would be conscious of his presence in their backyard soon enough. There was no need to telegraph the blow before it landed.

Hit and git. That was the plan. Grimaldi would be waiting to collect him at a preselected landing zone, a pinnacle of sorts amid the brooding forest, where a helicopter could land—or hover, at the very least—to take on passengers. It might be a hot LZ, if anything went wrong, but Grimaldi had plans to deal with that eventuality, as well.

Don't borrow trouble, Bolan thought. But planning for worst-case scenarios was part of waging any war. The fewer rude surprises a soldier faced, the longer he'd survive. The last thing Bolan needed, when he had a private army almost in his sights, was a bite from some stray reptile or arachnid.

At last the ground was visible and his descent accelerated. Ten more minutes and his boot soles touched solid ground for the first time since liftoff that morning, from Marechal Rondon International Airport in Várzea Grande. Bolan quickly shed his pack and combat gear, unzipped his jumpsuit and removed it, feeling cooler instantly. His combat webbing needed minor readjustment, with the thicker layer of clothing gone, but that was just a moment's work.

Keeping his Steyr close at hand, Bolan got busy with the Glock entrenching tool, digging a square grave for his jumpsuit and helmet. He kept the goggles pushed up on his forehead, as a hedge against flies, and buried the gear he was leaving behind. Once the shovel was folded and stowed, Bolan drank from one of his canteens, then donned his pack again.

Ready.

He knew where he was going, courtesy of satellite photography and the intelligence reports he'd received before departing from the States. His target wasn't secret in the normal sense. Brazil's army, its Federal Police and Mato Grosso's Civil Police Department knew the site's location and what it represented, but they made no moves against it.

Why? The answer might be corruption, preoccupation with domestic terrorism or simple fear of finding themselves outgunned. Most likely, Bolan thought, it was a combination of all three. He'd never seen a truly "clean" police force yet and was convinced he never would, since every agency on earth had to recruit its members from the human race.

Enter the Executioner, to do what these groups *could* not or *would* not bring themselves to try.

Bolan marked his path using the GPS and took off through the forest, rifle slung over his shoulder, bolo knife in hand. The animals he met were small and quick to clear out, in most cases before he could identify their species.

Perfect.

Then some twenty minutes in, he crossed a newly broken trail where something like a dozen men had passed in single file. Their destination seemed to be approximately the same as his, so he fell in step behind them.

Why not?

If he could trail the as-yet unknowns to the target, that was fine. If they began to deviate or stopped to rest along the way, Bolan could determine who they were, evaluate their strength and then decide whether they were a threat.

If they were enemies, as Bolan surmised, there was no point in letting this group rejoin their comrades, strengthening the hostile ranks. A dozen guns or so eliminated early in the game could only help Bolan later on.

Pleased with the turn of circumstance, he sheathed his bolo and unslung the Steyr AUG.

The Executioner was on the hunt.

2

Abner Cronin said a silent prayer of thanks when the raiding party stopped to rest. Two of the gunman shoved him and Mercy against the base of a towering tree and muttered something in Portuguese that he didn't catch. He'd learned the language fairly well—beginning his study when they'd hatched the plan to start a mission in Brazil—but there were many slang terms that eluded him, along with most of the profanity.

Why bother learning filth, when his intent was sharing scripture?

Sitting down was too much trouble with his hands bound tight behind his back, so Abner knelt to rest, and Mercy followed his example. The apparent leader of the kidnappers—a man who'd visited their mission once before and had warned them to move on—came over, frowning.

"You're praying now?" he asked them. Abner took his tone for curiosity, not outright mockery.

"Just resting," he replied. "Kneeling is recommended for prayer, but not required."

"Praying won't help you," said the gunman. "When you meet *o chefe*…" The guerrilla shook his head. "He is the last god you will ever see."

O chefe. That translated as "the boss." Abner decided he could take a chance, under the circumstances.

"No man is a god," he said.

"Maybe," the gunman answered. "But out here, he is the next best thing."

"Who is *o chefe?*" Abner asked. "And how have we offended him?"

"You don't know? Honestly?" Their captor croaked a laugh. "You never heard of Joaquim Braga?"

Abner frowned. The name *did* sound familiar, but—

Then it hit him. "The narco-trafficker?" he asked.

"Ah, so you *do* know him."

"We've heard of him," he answered, Mercy nodding in agreement. "But we've never met him. Certainly we've never interfered with any of his business."

"No?" The gunman shrugged. "Maybe he doesn't like you preaching Jesus to the natives, filling their heads with fairy tales."

"They aren't—"

"Or maybe he just wants you out of here. He don't like people snooping in his territory, running back to the police with stories, eh?"

"We don't know anything about his operation, and we have no dealings with police," Abner replied.

Their captor shrugged. "Is not for me to say. *O chefe* tells me, 'Go and bring the preachers back.' I bring you to him. Simple."

Abner was afraid to ask the next question but could not stop himself. "And so? What happens then?"

The gunman's smile was feral, verging on reptilian. "You talk to him, if he allows it. Maybe yes or no. You think it helps, try praying to him. Me, I think your time is running out."

A little sob came from Mercy, then quickly stifled. She was brave, and Abner loved her for it.

"We do not pray to any man," Abner replied.

Another lazy shrug followed. "It makes no difference

to me. Do what you want, eh? But *o chefe* don't like people
who stand up to him. They have a hard time crossing over."

Abner hoped it didn't show that he was trembling. "We
are not afraid," he lied.

"That's good. It makes a better show," the gunman said.
"And maybe at the end, you get to meet your Jesus, eh?"
He took some dried meat from a pocket of his cargo pants
and offered it to them. "You hungry?"

"What is that?" Mercy asked.

"Monkey meat. We dry it like your jerky. Pretty good."

"No. Thank you," Mercy said.

"No last meal, eh?"

Although he was hungry, Abner bit his tongue and
shook his head.

"Ho-kay." The gunman put his offering back in his
pocket and retreated, huddling with his soldiers farther
up the trail.

When he was gone, Abner told Mercy, "Please forgive
me."

"What? I don't—"

"None of this would be happening, except for me. I
brought us here and all for what?"

"To serve—"

"My ego," he said bitterly. "What have I done for anyone besides myself?"

"The mission, Abner. We—"

"Not *we*," he interrupted. "I trapped you into this. The
only woman I've ever loved, and now you're here, about
to die. Because of me."

"We can't give up," she answered. "Trust the Lord."

Abner swallowed the first retort that came to mind and
forced a smile. "You're right, of course," he said, but he
only half believed it. He could feel his own faith slipping,
sloughing off like old dead skin.

And now the leader of their enemies was doubling back

toward them. "Get up," he ordered in his rough, indifferent voice. "We're going now."

THE SIGHT OF prisoners surprised Mack Bolan. He'd been ready to take the small patrol by surprise until he saw the man and woman with their hands bound, being marched along at gunpoint. Spotting them, he scrubbed plan A and started looking for a way to liberate the captives with a minimum of danger. He'd counted twelve men dressed in camouflage besides the guy in charge.

A baker's dozen, ready for the oven.

Bolan saw his chance when they fell out to rest along the trail. A couple of the shooters wandered off to one side of the track, out of sight from their cronies, and Bolan went after them, drawing the silenced SIG Sauer P226. He moved as quietly as possible, counting on the jungle's constant background noise to cover what he had in mind.

Thinning the pack.

As he'd expected, the two men were answering the call of nature, situated several yards apart for something that approximated privacy. Bolan stood back and let them finish, listening as one man hassled the other, probably for taking too much time. Both were on their feet when Bolan hit them with a quick one-two, head shots from half a dozen paces that dropped them where they stood. A trace of crimson mist hung in the humid air, then settled on the corpses sprawled below.

Bolan rolled both bodies onto their backs and placed their autorifles lengthwise on their torsos, muzzles pointed toward their feet. Grabbing the first one's wrists, he dragged the shooter thirty feet or so, until Bolan reached a shallow gully in the woods and rolled the body into it. The second followed moments later, then Bolan circled back to spy on what remained of the patrol.

The soldiers hadn't noticed they were two men down,

as yet. Bolan wasn't entirely sure if anyone had watched the two depart, but Bolan assumed their people would be missed before the column started off again. Bolan had shaved the odds by 15 percent and now looked forward to the rest discovering their loss.

One of the remaining riflemen—Bolan had pegged him as the leader of the team—was talking to the prisoners. While Bolan wasn't close enough to eavesdrop, he could track the tenor of their conversation from the gunman's face and body language, and the attitude of his two kneeling captives. After they had rejected something from the gunner's pocket that resembled old shoe leather, the conversation petered out, with the raiding party's leader going back to join his men.

Bolan moved closer to the prisoners, letting the jungle and its shadows cover him until he reached the backside of the giant tree where they were kneeling, whispering together. Reaching them from where he crouched was perilous, for them as much as for himself. There was an outside chance that he could reach around the tree and slit their bonds without the shooters spotting him, but coming at the captives unaware was bound to set off some reaction from the hostages themselves, and that would kick the party off before Bolan was prepared. Better to leave the two prisoners where they were, for now.

The shooting, when it started, would be all around them. It was down to Bolan—his efficiency, his speed and skill— to make sure the hostages survived.

And then what?

He ignored that question for the moment, focused on the leader of the raiding party as he came back to his prisoners and said, in English, "Get up. We're going now."

LUIZ ARANHA WATCHED the missionaries struggle to their feet, not helping them. They'd been warned to leave the area and had ignored his words of caution. Now, within a few more hours, they would fully understand the price of their self-righteous arrogance.

He turned back to his men, milling about and clearly in no hurry to resume the march.

"Get in formation! This is not the time for slacking off!"

They grumbled but obeyed him, knowing that he spoke for *o chefe*. Their master's reputation might mean nothing to Bible-thumping meddlers from *dos Estados Unidos,* but the people of the Mato Grosso knew and feared the power of Joaquim Braga. That fear would have his soldiers marching through the jungle till their feet were bloody, if need be. None would dare defy *o chefe* and expect to live another day.

"Where are Carlos and Abílio?" asked someone from the ranks.

Aranha scanned the line of men in camouflage, the prisoners now in their place, with guns before them and behind. He counted heads, came up with ten and mouthed a curse.

"*Filho da puta!* Who saw where they went?"

No one replied. Some of his soldiers shrugged and shook their heads.

"Someone must have seen them! Anybody?"

More shrugs. His men were getting nervous as Aranha moved along the line, glaring at each in turn.

"Carlos said he had to piss," one of them finally admitted.

"What of Abílio?" Aranha challenged. "Did he go along to hold his *piru* for him?"

Farther down the line, another of Aranha's soldiers said, "He also had to go, I think."

"Well, how long does it take, *por amor de Cristo?*"

No one answered that. Aranha turned to face the forest, shouting out, "Carlos! Abílio! *Onde você está?*"

The jungle's only answer was a monkey screeching somewhere overhead.

"All right," Aranha told the others. "Find them. Teams of two. Hurry!"

Grudgingly his men fanned out, pairs moving off into the woods on both sides of the narrow trail. Aranha watched them disappear into the shadows, calling to their comrades and getting no response. Aranha shifted closer to the prisoners, keeping them covered with his rifle as if they might suddenly decide to make a run for freedom.

Where had the fools gone? How could they possibly get lost, mere paces from the trail they had been following? One man, perhaps—but two? It was ridiculous and, yet, no joking matter. Aranha was losing valuable time, falling behind his schedule, which would not amuse *o chefe*. The responsibility fell on Aranha's shoulders, and if he faced punishment for tardiness, he meant to have Abílio and Carlos on the block beside him.

The prisoners were silent, standing with their backs against the tree where they'd been kneeling moments earlier. They watched Aranha apprehensively, perhaps reading his mood and understanding that the slightest thing could make Aranha snap. His fingers ached from clutching his rifle too tightly, and Aranha loosened them deliberately, willing himself to relax.

But still… What could have happened to his men?

Assume the worst. If they had stumbled on a nest of bushmasters and suffered fatal bites, they still could have returned before the venom took effect. If they had panicked, fleeing in the wrong direction, then Aranha should have heard their cries for help. A jaguar might have taken one, but not the pair of them—and not without a noisy fight.

It was the silent disappearance that unnerved Aranha. There was something almost supernatural about it, though he mocked subordinates for clinging to such superstitions. Witches, ghosts and demons in the forest were the stuff of children's stories. Many things were lethal in the Amazon, but all of them were made of flesh and blood.

"Come on. Hurry," Aranha muttered to himself.

And then the shooting started.

THE PLAN WAS simple in conception, not so much in execution. Bolan had the raiders eyeballed as their leader gave the order to disperse and find their missing comrades. Two-man teams moved out, ten soldiers altogether. Two teams scouted on the west side of the trail, three on the east. Their honcho stayed behind, of course, to guard the prisoners.

So far, so good.

Bolan had started with a full twenty-round magazine in his SIG Sauer P226, plus one round in the chamber. He was two down now, which left nineteen silent rounds to go before he had to switch out magazines. Eleven targets meant he had shots to spare, if everything went smoothly.

The first search team on Bolan's side of the game trail was easy. They were put out by the extra duty, muttering about it between their calls for Carlos and Abílio. Bolan came up behind them, gave them each a Parabellum shocker to the head and put them down. No muss, no fuss. The earth soaked up their blood, and hungry flies were circling over them before he'd cleared the killing site.

Nine left.

The other team on Bolan's side had gone to the northwest, whooping for their friends who couldn't answer. Bolan trailed them, picking up his pace to overtake the pair, knowing their voices must be audible back on the trail. If he could take them down, then cross the path and circle back to find the other searchers, he would have a decent chance of pulling off a sweep.

If nothing went awry.

And, of course, it did.

A hundred yards or so from where they'd started, Bolan's latest targets stopped to catch their breath. Bolan closed the gap then, dropping one while they were lighting cigarettes, the other still gaping as his friend went down, blood pouring from his shattered skull. Before the second guy could turn and raise his weapon, Bolan drilled a bullet through his temple. It was quick and clean—but the man's index finger clenched on the trigger of his automatic rifle.

Half a dozen rounds went off before the dead man fell and dropped his weapon. None of them were aimed at Bolan, ripping harmlessly through shrubs and ferns, but the staccato would be audible to anyone nearby.

So much for stealth.

He turned and ran in the direction of the trail, reached it as voices started shouting back and forth through forest shadows, calling for a sitrep. Bolan wasn't sure how well they could triangulate on the brief burst of gunfire, but he knew his best hope of rolling up the kidnap team meant intercepting them in pairs, before they reassembled.

Seven survivors, six of them paired off, and all on full alert. All armed with quality assault rifles, presumably well versed in using them. The last thing he could do was take an easy blitz for granted, but he couldn't let the odds intimidate him, either. Not if he intended to come out of this on top and keep the hostages alive.

Crossing the trail, Bolan holstered his SIG and slipped the Steyr AUG off its shoulder sling, thumbing the fire-selector switch to semiautomatic mode. He'd noted that the hostiles' rifles were the same caliber as his, permitting Bolan to take advantage of a marginal confusion factor in the jungle murk. If they had been armed with Kalashnikovs, for instance, anyone could tell the difference between his weapon firing and the home team's.

As it was, however…

Bolan overtook the third pair as they backtracked toward the game trail. He shot them and ducked away before the rest could move in on the latest sound of gunfire. When he heard the others thrashing toward him, two additional pairs rapidly converging, he squeezed off a single shot in each direction, then ducked and let the fireworks fly.

Full-auto madness ripped through the jungle. Screams of pain and shouts of anger followed as the shots struck home. Another moment's wait before the Executioner moved in and started mopping up.

MERCY CRONIN COULDN'T fathom what was happening. Their rest stop had become a waking nightmare, worse— if such a thing was even possible—than the abduction that had preceded it. She had been praying and preparing to meet death with what she'd hoped would be dignity and courage when the leader of their kidnappers discovered that a couple of his men were missing. Moments later there was shooting in the forest, first from one side of the trail and then the other.

What on earth was happening? Was this some kind of ambush? And if so, who was responsible?

Of greater interest to her—what did it mean for Abner and herself?

She knew there had been revolutionary groups throughout Brazil during the country's period of military rule, from 1964 to 1985. Most had disbanded with the restoration of civilian government, but isolated factions still remained at large, existing now as bandits rather than political commandos. There were also right-wing death squads, but they operated chiefly in the urban jungles of Brazil, São Paulo and Rio de Janeiro, and were—or so she'd heard—composed of rogue policemen. Neither seemed likely to attack a column of narco-trafficker gun-men in the midst of the Amazon Basin.

Who then?

She also ruled out guardian angels, who could have struck down her abductors with their blinding light of righteousness without resorting to earthly weapons. No, human beings were involved—but who? And why?

The leader of their kidnappers had crouched behind them when the shooting started, jabbing his rifle's muzzle into Mercy's ribs. After some filthy oaths in Portuguese, he had said, "You better hope my men come out on top. Somebody comes for me, you both are dead meat, eh?"

Tears brimmed in Mercy's eyes, but she refused to let him see her trembling. Abner leaned a little to his right, pressing his arm against her own, and Mercy found the contact comforting. He couldn't save her, obviously, but at least they were together and would face their fate as one.

Off to her right, along the east side of the trail, the gun-fire sputtered out at last. A sobbing cry of pain warbled through ringing silence, then the normal forest sounds began returning gradually, filling in the quiet. Mercy waited, her gaze sweeping the tree line, trying to imagine what would happen next.

Nothing could have prepared her for the sight of a lone man stepping from the shadows, dressed in camouflage and battle clad, his face painted with stripes of black and green. She guessed he was six feet tall or thereabouts. The rifle in his hands was smaller than her captor's weapon, and it looked peculiar to her, but it seemed no less deadly.

"The hell are you?" her kidnapper demanded, speaking English.

"Last man standing," the stranger said.

"You kill all my soldiers, eh?"

"Some of them killed each other."

"*Idiotas*. They deserve it then."

No answer came from the new arrival.

"So, whatchoo want?" asked the last of Mercy's kid-nappers.

The stranger nodded toward her and Abner and said, "I'll take them off your hands."

"You think so, eh?"

"They're more than you can handle."

"Not so hard to kill, though."

"Maybe not. But then, who covers you?"

"You like the cowboy movies, eh? *High Noon?*"

The stranger casually checked his watch and said, "Not quite."

"I like you, man. Too bad I have to kill you soon."

"Why wait?" the tall man asked—and then his rifle cracked, a single shot, and Mercy gasped as something wet and warm spattered her cheek. The leader tumbled over backward, kicked her with a dying spasm of his leg and then lay still.

"You two all right?" the painted gunman asked as he approached them.

"I...I think so," Abner answered. "Who are you?"

"A friend."

The tall man drew a vicious-looking knife, brass knuck-les on its handle, as he stepped around behind them. Mercy braced herself for lancing pain, eyes closed, then felt the blade slice through the plastic binding that had secured her wrists. A moment later, Abner's hands were freed, as well. The wicked knife was sheathed before the stranger stepped in front of them again.

"Now, if you're fit to walk," he said, "we need to get away from here, ASAP."

3

Condor Acampamento, Mato Grosso

Joaquim Braga lounged behind his desk in air-conditioned comfort while the jungle sweltered only feet away. His combination living quarters and command post was a four-room prefab bungalow that had been airlifted to his compound. Each room was chilled by its own window unit, powered by one of the camp's six generators. With his eyes closed, it was sometimes possible for Braga to forget that he was living in the middle of the wilderness.

But not today.

Across his desk, reclining in a leather-padded captain's chair, his guest from Bogotá looked tense, verging on irritated. Not a good thing, considering the power he represented and his importance to the Braga syndicate.

"Is something troubling you, *meu amigo?*" Braga asked.

Hugo Cardona exhaled, not quite disguising his sigh. "I had supposed your people would be back by now, to start the entertainment."

"Such delays are not uncommon in the Mato Grosso, as I'm sure you understand," Braga replied. "I've sent a pair of scouts to locate the patrol and hurry it along."

"Of course. Perhaps I overestimated the efficiency of operations in such a primitive environment."

"How is your vodka, by the way?" Braga asked. "Cold enough?"

"It's adequate," Cardona said. "My brand, in fact. Diva."

"Is it?"

Of course it was. Braga had done his homework for this meeting, as he did for every significant event.

"How did you come to name this place…what is it?"

"*Condor Acampamento*," Braga said. "Camp Condor. It is named for Operation Condor. You remember it?"

Cardona mulled it over for a moment. He sipped his vodka and shook his head.

"It was before your time, perhaps. A covert operation undertaken by my country with the governments of Argentina, Chile, Paraguay, Bolivia and Uruguay. Encouraged by the CIA, of course—but then, what isn't, in our corner of the world?"

"They have been helpful with our shipments in the past," Cardona granted.

"Winning hearts and minds. With Operation Condor, they attempted to eradicate the Left from South America entirely, plus a host of other undesirables. Trade unions and rebellious students, troublesome reporters and environmentalists. The estimate of eighty thousand dead or disappeared, I think, is quite conservative."

"You named your home-away-from-home after a genocide campaign?"

"Not genocide," Braga corrected him. "Cleansing. My parents were among those who disgraced themselves and were eliminated. Thankfully I was adopted by a colonel and his barren wife, given advantages I never would have had with those who had spawned me."

"Fascinating," Cardona said.

"Do you think so? On the day I came of age and first had access to the fortune my adoptive father had looted from the thousands he had killed, I took his head with a

machete, gave it to his bitch wife for their anniversary
and watched her lose her mind. She lived another eighteen
months, as a drooling vegetable in São Paulo's cheapest
rat hole for the mentally defective."

"A cautionary tale, I'm sure. About these missionaries…"

"Meddlers from up north. They're a minor irritation,
but I will not suffer any interference with my operations."

"That is reassuring. When the shipment comes tomorrow—"

Urgent knocking on the door distracted Braga. "Excuse
me, *por favor*," he said, then barked, "Enter!"

His second in command, Oswaldo Ramos, stepped into
the office space of Braga's bungalow. "Apologies."

"Well, what is it?" Braga demanded.

"The scouts are back."

"And the patrol?"

"Ambushed," Ramos told him. "Wiped out."

"What?! What are you saying?"

"*Morto*," Ramos said. "Shot down to the last man."

"What of the *missionários?*"

"Gone. Not among the dead."

Braga could feel the heat of anger rising in his cheeks
and made a conscious effort to repress it. Rising from behind his desk, he told Ramos, "I'll see the scouts myself."

"Of course. They're just outside."

And so they were, two worried-looking soldiers damp
with sweat and intermittent rain. They stood before Braga
with eyes downcast and told their story of discovering
Luiz Aranha and his troops gunned down, their flyblown
corpses decomposing swiftly in the jungle's heat and sti-
fling humidity. They had been wise enough to bring back
the dead men's rifles, which confused Braga. Whether his
soldiers had been ambushed by police or bandits, he as-

sumed the victors in that skirmish would have made off
with their weapons.

"And no sign of the American missionaries?" he
pressed.

"No, boss," they said, not quite in unison.

"But Luiz and the others were returning from the mission."

They exchanged a glance and nodded, one—on Braga's
left—saying, "We think so."

"Then the missionaries must be found," Braga said.
Looking at the sky above the clearing where his compound stood, he frowned at the approach of night. "Tomorrow morning, each of you will lead a new patrol to
seek them out. In fact, I will send three to search the forest. No one rests, no one returns, without *os missionários.
Você entende?*"

Both men nodded, whereupon Braga sent them off to
feed themselves and rest. Tomorrow, at first light, they
would go hunting.

And God help them if they came back empty-handed.

Missão Misericórdia

RETURNING TO THE mission was a waste of time and energy,
in Bolan's view, but the two prisoners he'd rescued were
adamant about discovering how many of their congregants
had fallen during the attack. It was easier to join them on
the trek back to their jungle church than to debate it. Bolan
used the time to think about arranging their extraction.

Jack Grimaldi was available, but night would fall before
he could prepare the helicopter he had on standby for unexpected rescue missions. That meant waiting until daybreak,
and the Cronins had agreed with Bolan that spending all
night at the mission would be tantamount to suicide. Another raiding party might arrive at any time, once Bolan's

eradication of the first one was discovered, and a single glance had told Bolan that their Mercy Mission had not been constructed with defense in mind.

Arriving on the scene, they found no bodies. Bolan did not share the surprise of Abner Cronin and his wife, knowing that it was typical of aborigines to claim their dead and spirit them away. Bloodstains were visible where some had fallen, swarming now with ants and flies, but the Cronins would likely never know how many had been slain, how many wounded. Every jungle on the planet had its secrets.

The hike back from the killing ground to Mercy Mission had been tense at first. In answer to the Cronins' questions, Bolan had introduced himself as Matthew Cooper and left his ties to Washington deliberately vague. If they'd had assumed he was CIA or DEA, so be it. He had informed them that his business in Brazil involved Joaquim Braga and that their rescue was a mere coincidence.

Abner had disagreed on that point, claiming the Lord had moved and motivated Bolan, whether Bolan was aware of it or not. Mercy, for her part, could not seem to get her mind around the killings she'd witnessed, and she'd looked askance at Bolan while they marched, as if he might decide to shoot her and her husband on a whim.

Arriving at the mission had distracted her from that fear, for the moment, as she searched in vain for bodies and examined the damage caused by the attackers. Abner trailed her, Bolan hanging back and watching from a distance as they viewed the ruin of their dream. He knew the pang of loss but also hoped they realized they were lucky to be alive.

They chose to view the incident as "a miracle."

When they'd gathered whichever belongings fit into their backpacks, they returned to Bolan, waiting for instructions. "I can't get you out tonight," he said, "but I'll arrange an airlift for the morning. In the meantime, we need to get away from here and find someplace safe to put up for the night that's close to the LZ."

"LZ?" Mercy echoed.

"Landing zone," her husband translated. "And there's no place to land a plane out here. The nearest airport would be in Cáceres."

"I was thinking of a helicopter," Bolan said. "Two sites selected. We can get an early start and try the nearest of them first. If that falls through, we'll still have time to reach the second."

"And tonight?" Mercy asked.

"No fire, I'm afraid," Bolan said, "but I do have MREs with flameless heaters."

"We'd best be going then," Abner observed, "before it's dark."

"Sounds like a plan," Bolan agreed, and took the lead into the jungle as day edged toward night.

Condor Acampamento

HUGO CARDONA HAD auditioned for the Medellín Cartel when he was just fourteen years old. The task was simple and had not required much talent on his part, only the kind of nerve that makes a soldier great. He'd been handed a pistol—he still remembered it, a .45-caliber Colt M1911—and told to execute a random stranger on the street. He had exceeded expectations, walking up behind a couple on vacation from West Germany and killing them both, firing all seven rounds at point-blank range.

Over the next nine years, before the National Police had cornered Pablo Escobar and executed him, Cardona had eliminated sixty-seven people, rising through the ranks as he displayed intelligence to match his ruthless courage. When the cartel crumbled, he'd made his way to Bogotá with nineteen million dollars looted from its treasury and started fresh, selecting partners he could trust—at least, as long as they were terrified of him—and prospered hugely as a narco-trafficker. His product line had been expanded from cocaine alone to include heroin, marijuana and methamphetamine, supplying customers in the United States, Canada and Europe.

In the process, Cardona had discovered Brazil. It was the world's second-largest consumer of cocaine—after America—a major cannabis producer, a way station for airborne drug shipments between Colombia and Peru, with Rio de Janeiro being a primary transshipment point for drugs en route to Europe. Furthermore financial institutions in Rio and São Paulo laundered millions of dollars in narco profits per month.

All of which combined to place Cardona in the Mato Grosso jungle at this moment, watching Joaquim Braga try to recoup from the ambush that had cost him thirteen men.

Cardona's bond with Braga was a relatively new relationship. Thus far it had been profitable, but his first major delivery to Braga—one thousand kilos of cocaine aboard a Sikorsky UH-60M BLACK HAWK helicopter—was scheduled to occur tomorrow afternoon. Cardona hoped that Braga's current trouble would not interfere with business, but that remained to be seen.

"I will find them in the morning," Braga told Cardona, as they sat down to eat. "They cannot elude my soldiers in the jungle."

"Even with help?" Cardona asked before taking his first mouthful of *feijoada,* a delicious stew of beef, pork and beans.

Braga was starting with *moqueca*—slow-cooked fish, tomato, onion and garlic, topped with cilantro. He paused with the spoon halfway to his lips and said, "I'll find the men responsible, as well. Before the merchandise arrives, you'll see their heads strung up to decorate the camp."

"It should be most instructive," Cardona said. "I look forward to it."

"And when that is done, perhaps you'd like to join in hunting Mundurukus? There aren't many left, but they make good sport."

"Perhaps," Cardona said. He had no qualms about hunting a forest tribe for pleasure—it might be a nice diversion—but he always dealt with business first. "How many men will you send out tomorrow?"

"I suppose three teams of twenty," Braga said. "Still leaving seventy with us. You'll be secure, Hugo. I promise you."

"Of course."

Cardona, who had flown into the jungle camp with six men of his own, was less concerned about himself than his incoming merchandise. The massacre of Braga's men was troublesome, but long experience had taught him that such things were bound to happen in the course of doing business. Soldiers were a cheap commodity and easily replaced.

Trust in a colleague, on the other hand, was rare and fragile. Whether his relationship with Braga flourished or was snatched up by the roots would now depend on how Joaquim made up for his recent loss.

"WHAT DO YOU think of him?" Mercy asked, barely whispering to Abner as they ate their evening meal. The man who called himself Matt Cooper was out of earshot, speaking to someone by satellite phone to arrange their extraction, but Mercy was taking no chances.

"I'm not sure yet," her husband answered. "He's a man of violence obviously, but I don't believe he means to harm us."

Mercy had already reached the same conclusion—why

would Cooper have helped them otherwise?—but there
was still something about him that unnerved her. So much
killing, with no indication whatsoever that it had disturbed
him.

On the other hand, he'd fed them well. And the MREs
were surprisingly good: lemon pepper tuna and garlic mashed potatoes for Mercy, chili and macaroni with
Santa Fe rice for Abner. Each MRE included a flameless
heater—a thin, flexible pad about the size of a playing card
that contained salt, iron dust and magnesium dust. Add-
ing water brought the mixture to a boil, and its insertion
into the MRE pouch produced a hot meal in ten minutes,
without a trace of telltale smoke or flame.

"Who do you think he's calling?" Mercy asked.

"Somebody from the government, I'd bet," Abner replied. "Could be the embassy or one of the consulates.
Any of them could connect him to the CIA. There's also
the Marine Corps detachment in São Paulo."

"What do you think about him finding us that way, by
accident?"

"You know I don't believe in accidents," Abner said.
"Everything that happens is God's will, whether we understand His aims or not."

"Of course, but—"

"We've been rescued by the Lord," he interrupted her,
"in order to continue with our mission."

"What? After all that's happened here today?"

"We knew there would be dangers, Mercy. We discussed this time and time again, before we left Miami."

"Yes, I know, but—"

"We rely on faith," he interrupted her. "Did the apostles
shrink away from peril as they spread the word? Surely
our risk is no greater than theirs."

Mercy thought about the twelve apostles, frowning. Ac-
cording to tradition, only one of them—Saint John—had

lived a full life and expired from natural causes. Ten had been martyred, most by crucifixion, and everyone knew what had happened to Judas.

"I understand," she said. "But is it wise to stay on when we know men are trying to kill us?"

"Mercy, wisdom is—"

"I know, I know."

"You seem discouraged."

There's a revelation for you, Mercy thought. Instead, she said, "We've just been kidnapped, Abner. I'm convinced we would be dead by now, if not for Mr. Cooper."

"Praise be to God! He rescued us so that we can continue with our work."

"Or to suggest we may have been mistaken in the first place."

"After all our prayers and preparation? Don't you think He would have sent a sign dissuading us, if that was His intent?"

Mercy wasn't convinced that God always responded to requests for guidance. Truth be told, sometimes she wasn't even certain that He listened, but she couldn't voice that kind of doubt to Abner. It was not her role in life to shake his faith. Scripture admonished women to be "discreet, chaste, keepers at home, good, obedient to their own husbands, that the word of God be not blasphemed."

All right, so some of that might sound old-fashioned, even medieval, but who was she to question God's instructions? It boiled down to the matter of Abner's calling. If he had truly been summoned by God to serve the Amazon natives, it would be treacherous for her to undermine Abner's confidence.

But what if he was mistaken?

She knew that some ministers *thought* they'd been

called by the Lord, when in fact they had not. Isaiah, Jeremiah, Amos—all the great biblical prophets had experienced dramatic callings, whereas Abner…well, sometimes she thought he had *decided* they should launch a foreign ministry, without firm guidance from their Savior.

No. She stopped herself. That can't be right. She knew Abner too well, loved him too much, to doubt him now. But she was frightened of remaining in the jungle. Call it weakness in herself, a lapse of faith, whatever. Mercy Cronin knew only one thing with any certainty.

She wanted out.

Condor Acampamento

OSWALDO RAMOS CHOSE a soldier from the ranks to lead one of the three patrols the next morning, along with the two scouts already appointed by Braga to each lead a team. *O chefe* wanted twenty men in each search party, sweeping different sectors of the forest. One would march back to the site where their comrades had been slaughtered and proceed from there to the mission run by the missing Americans. Two others would travel in different directions, east and west of the mission, searching for signs of the fugitives and whoever had delayed the missionaries' punishment for meddling on *o chefe*'s turf.

The preachers had done nothing wrong, per se. Not yet. But Ramos understood his master's reason for eliminating them. They were potential witnesses to various illegal operations, in their own right, and their tampering with native minds had the potential to encourage opposition to the Braga syndicate among the forest tribes. When the couple was dead—and, better yet, displayed as an example to potential future interlopers—order would be restored.

Except now it seemed some outside force had intervened to help them, killing thirteen of the syndicate's enlisted sol-

diers. Ramos had already racked his brain in vain attempts
to work out who might be responsible for the attack. So far
he had ruled out the army's Jungle Infantry Brigade, the
Federal Police and the Mato Grosso Civil Police.

Each of those agencies was ruthless enough to kill
Braga's men, and while they might have left the corpses
scattered in the jungle, none would have abandoned automatic weapons. Furthermore Ramos had personally bribed
some of the highest-ranking law enforcement officers in
Mato Grosso to protect *o chefe*'s operations, and there'd
been no trouble from them previously.

Well, no trouble without ample warning.

No, this was something—someone—else.

He wished that a single individual had survived from
the original patrol, to offer a description of the enemy. If
they were has-been rebels turned to banditry, the argument
about collecting weapons from the dead would still apply.

But if they'd been foreigners…

Who might conspire against *o chefe* from the outside
world? Competitors, perhaps—which could include Russian traffickers, seeking to hold the European market; cartels from Santa Cruz supported by Serb mercenaries; or
one of the Mexican cartels that envied Braga's growing
share of the American drug trade. None of those would
bother to collect the guns from rivals they shot down, since
their own arsenals were vast, sources essentially unlimited.

Ramos did not enjoy the prospect of a war against one
of their major rivals, particularly since the battleground
would now encompass half the planet. Even if they only
fought within Brazil and the United States, he could expect
a rise in violence to prompt more energetic crackdowns
by authorities. A war was always bad for business, but
the industry was fraught with mayhem. Look at Mexico,
where estimates of drug-related homicides over the past
few years were in the tens of thousands.

And yet the cartels still banked their billions, held their funerals and forged ahead with business. When a leader fell, he was replaced, and life went on—for some.

A notion came to Ramos, not for the first time. His own ambition had been stifled by Braga's dominance, and while Ramos could not logically complain about the wealth he had accumulated in the service of *o chefe,* Ramos always yearned for…more. If war broke out, it was not difficult to picture Braga falling in the struggle, and who better to replace him than his loyal second in command?

Something to think about. But first, beginning at dawn, he had to launch the three patrols in search of the Americans and whoever had been fool enough to fight on their behalf. Examples needed to be made, a lesson taught to all prospective rivals.

And when *that* was finished, Ramos could begin to think about his own prospects.

4

Várzea Grande, Mato Grosso

Jack Grimaldi's hotel room was small and musty smelling. Not the worst he'd ever stayed in, but among the bottom few, for sure. There was an eight-inch gecko clinging to one wall, but he hadn't disturbed it, on the theory that it might intimidate whatever other creepy-crawlers were lurking out of sight, waiting for him to douse the lamps and kill the television.

Not that watching it provided much, in terms of entertainment. He could only get four channels, three of them in Portuguese, the fourth some kind of time warp to the 1950s with a nonstop offering of *I Love Lucy, Death Valley Days, Have Gun—Will Travel* and *Alfred Hitchcock Presents.* Still it could have been worse. The new music video channel, for example, rife with "reality" shows about teens in New Jersey and no music at all.

The sat phone rescued him from Lucy's foray into bottling salad dressing, losing money on each jar but "making it up in volume." He answered midway through the first ring, knowing it meant trouble for a call to come this soon.

"What happened?" he inquired, by way of salutation.

Bolan's voice came through the scrambled link. "I've picked up a couple stragglers. Long story. They need to exit in the morning."

Grimaldi didn't argue, didn't bother identifying potential problems with the schedule they had laid out in advance. He said, "Okay. Just tell me where and when."

"The first LZ we marked," Bolan replied. "I'd like to get them out around first light. If we run into any problems there, I'll call and redirect to the second."

Grimaldi had the topographic map memorized. The landing zones they had selected, A and B, were clearings in the forest, higher ground than was normal for the area. Grimaldi didn't know why they were both devoid of trees, but satellite photography had confirmed it. Either place, he would have room to set down a chopper, take passengers on board and lift them out.

Whether the LZ turned up hot was something else entirely. In that case, he would have to count on Bolan and his own resources, if he wanted to survive.

"I'll be there," Grimaldi assured his friend. "First light."

"Then we reset and go ahead with Braga," Bolan told him.

"Works for me."

"Tomorrow then."

"Tomorrow," Grimaldi confirmed, before the line clicked dead.

Tomorrow hadn't always been a sure thing for Grimaldi. He'd been flying for the Mafia when Bolan had skyjacked him—could just as well have iced him—but they'd hit it off despite the adverse circumstances. Somewhere in the midst of praying that he'd live another day, Grimaldi had enlisted in the warrior's lonely struggle—had become Bolan's one-man air force, in effect—and after Bolan had faked his death to join the covert team at Stony Man Farm, in Virginia, Grimaldi had followed to become a member, as well.

He'd seen the world, and then some, flying for the mob and then for Bolan. Grimaldi had been places that most people only read about or glimpsed in passing on the Travel Channel, but he hadn't led a tourist's life by any means. Along with vistas that could take his breath away, there had been situations that would've stopped his breath for good, if he had allowed himself a heartbeat's hesitation in the crunch.

Grimaldi didn't just deliver Bolan to a combat zone and pick him up again when all the dirty work was done. Grimaldi was a warrior of the skies, with a prodigious body count, although he tried to think in terms of helping others, not just wreaking havoc on a faceless enemy.

Bolan had mentioned *stragglers,* plural, whatever that meant. Bolan had a penchant for snatching strangers out of tight places, even when it put Bolan's life and his mission at risk. Grimaldi had no idea what to expect, beyond a dawn flight to retrieve the latest strays. There'd been no mention of a medevac, so Grimaldi assumed that the two were fit to travel, and more or less intact. Beyond that... well, the places Bolan deployed were generally not conducive to the best of health.

Grimaldi would be up and out by 2:00 a.m. to get the waiting helicopter ready for its rescue mission. Until then, he would dispense with loving Lucy and attempt to get some sleep.

God only knew when he would get another chance.

Cold Camp, Mato Grosso

BOLAN REJOINED THE Cronins as they finished up their MREs. "It's set," he told them. "You'll be flying out at first light, from a spot about two miles northeast of here. Allowing for terrain, we'll need to start the hike at three o'clock. The best thing you can do right now is try to get some rest."

"Will you be flying with us?" Mercy asked him.

"No. I still have work to do. But I'll be leaving you in good hands, and you'll be delivered to authorities that you can trust."

"Americans?" asked Abner.

"Likely someone from the consulate," Bolan replied.

"And will they send us back?"

"Smart money says they'll recommend a change of scene. They don't have the authority to drag you home without an extradition warrant. Now if the Brazilians get involved, there's no predicting what may happen."

"Meaning they could deport us."

Mercy tugged his sleeve. "Abner, maybe it's best—"

"I want to get this straight," he cut her off. "Our mission could be sacrificed, through no fault of our own?"

"You'll have to talk that over with whoever meets you in Várzea Grande," Bolan said. "I won't pretend to be a diplomat."

"It isn't fair," Abner complained to no one in particular, while Mercy took his hand and tried to soothe him silently.

"I'll say again that you should try to get some sleep," Bolan said. "When I get back—"

"Back from where?" Mercy asked, sounding worried now.

"I have some place to go tonight," he said. "Some things I have to check on."

"But…you're leaving us?"

"You should be fine. Braga won't have another hunting party out tonight, and I'll be back by one o'clock."

"What if…you aren't?"

"I will be," Bolan reassured her. "Recon only. Just sit tight, no fire. If it feels better to you, sleep in shifts."

He left them with his Maglite and the adjustable Glock entrenching tool, which could double as a hoe— or hatchet—if a viper happened by during the night. He cautioned them to use the flashlight sparingly, as much to keep from drawing insects or attention to themselves as to preserve its batteries.

"What if someone *does* come?" Mercy asked when he was prepared to leave.

"They won't," Bolan said. "First, Braga's men already took a beating in broad daylight, and he won't like risking any more of them at night, if he can help it. Second, he knows they wouldn't stand a chance of tracking us, now that it's dark. The only place they know to look for you is at the mission."

"The mission!" Abner said. "What if the Mundurukus come back to find us?"

"Unlikely," Bolan told him. "I'd imagine that they're smart enough to stay away from Braga's people and from government patrols by now. They lost people today and saw you carried off. Most likely they assume you're dead."

"I still believe the mission means something to them," Abner insisted. "We've been getting through to them. Sharing the word."

"Let's say you're right," Bolan allowed. "Without you, Mercy Mission's just another empty building. By this time next month, the jungle will have started to reclaim it. Life goes on."

"But what about salvation?" Abner challenged. "We were making progress! And the Mundurukus still have much to learn."

Bolan was losing time and patience with the preacher. "Listen, if you want to stick around after tomorrow, make your case to someone from the consulate. Just stay away until I'm finished here. The day after tomorrow should be fine."

"What are you doing?" Mercy asked him.

"Not your problem. All you need to know is that you're in the line of fire if you stay here. You caught a lucky break today, but that's unusual. Don't count on two."

"You don't believe in miracles?" She sounded disappointed.

"I believe in preparation and determination," Bolan said. *And firepower.*

"You lead a lonely life."

"Works better that way, all around. Now, if there's nothing else?"

First Mercy, then her husband, shook their heads. Bolan left them, moving off into the darkness, heading for the initial glimpse of his enemy.

Várzea Grande, Mato Grosso

THE HELICOPTER WAS a vintage Bell UH-1 Iroquois, widely known as a Huey, officially retired from military service but still full of life—and fight. Jack Grimaldi, after power-napping in his lizard room at the hotel, had made his way to Marechal Rondon International Airport for a preflight checkup on the chopper. He felt better on the tarmac than he would have lying on his saggy rented bed and watching Richard Boone or James Arness taming the West that never was.

Grimaldi liked the Huey. A single Lycoming T53-L-11 turboshaft engine powered the bird, with a cruising speed of 125 miles per hour, and 10 miles per hour on top of that for maximum speed. As it sat before him now, the chopper was unarmed.

In combat, it would carry the M21 weapons subsytem, mounted externally, with each side of the aircraft sporting a seven-tube launcher loaded with 2.75-inch folding-fin rockets otherwise known as the "mighty mouse," plus an M134 minigun chambered in 7.62 mm NATO.

Each of the six-barrel Gatling-type weapons had a selectable fire-rate capability ranging from two thousand to four thousand rounds per minute. Grimaldi had the M21 setup in storage, but it was a two-man job to mount it on the helicopter, and from what Bolan had told Grimaldi on the sat phone, heavy hardware would not be required for his pickup at dawn.

Not that Grimaldi would be flying naked when he retrieved Bolan's newfound friends. Grimaldi would be carrying a Heckler & Koch UMP—the company's *U*niversal *M*achine *P*istol—in .40 S&W, with an H&K USP semi-auto pistol in the same caliber as backup. Nothing heavy, granted, and he wasn't hauling any spare survival gear beyond a standard first-aid kit.

As he completed his preflight check, Grimaldi couldn't help speculating about his passengers. So far he only knew the obvious—that there were two of them, and Bolan had not counted on them when he had hatched their master plan to tackle Joaquim Braga in his own backyard. They were an unknown quantity and, therefore, hazardous.

The green light for the Braga operation had come down from Stony Man Farm, in Virginia, meaning Hal Brognola, back at the U.S. Department of Justice. Braga was on the map as someone who had proven to be untouchable. A modern warlord on the level of opium kingpin Khun Sa in the Golden Triangle.

Braga had his own private army—though it hadn't reached the size of Khun Sa's Mong Tai Army, boasting twenty thousand men at peak strength—and Braga was shielded from attempts at extradition by a network of corrupt police, judges and politicians in Brazil.

Enter the Executioner.

It was the kind of job Bolan did best, almost a patented specialty. Penetration of a hardsite no one else could breach, and elimination of the target and whoever chose to stand in his defense, plus whatever contraband was readily accessible. A quick job, in and out.

Until somebody dropped a pair of innocent civilians into the mix.

What were they doing in the middle of the Amazon rain forest, much less blocking Bolan's field of fire? Grimaldi reckoned he would find out soon enough, and in the meantime, it would do no good for him to speculate. Bolan had set a task for Grimaldi, and he would do it to the best of his ability.

And in Grimaldi's case, when it came down to flying rescue missions, that was pretty goddamned good.

Cold Camp, Mato Grosso

IT WAS ABNER Cronin's turn on watch, the first time since his very early days in the Brazilian wilderness that he'd stayed awake and listened to the jungle around him. It was strange how soon a city boy got used to things like that and started taking them for granted. Oh, he'd trained himself to shake his shoes and check his clothing every morning, just in case some uninvited visitor had dropped in overnight, but he had quickly lost his fear of walking, working, living in the forest's majesty.

Until tonight.

Tonight, he was embarking on a perilous adventure unlike any in the past. And he was going it alone.

For some time now, Abner had been aware of Mercy's faltering commitment to their mission in the jungle. She had gone through all the motions, made the right contented sounds; but after fourteen years of marriage, he knew Mercy well enough to recognize when she had lost her zeal for a project. He had seen it happen in Miami, with a couple of the charities they'd served; and he'd recognized the same signs when their life in the Brazilian rain forest had begun to wear her down. To Mercy's credit, she had not complained—not verbally—but her increasing weariness was evident.

Still Abner might have managed to rejuvenate her, somehow, if it had not been for Braga's men. The threats were bad enough, but the attack had finished her. He saw that clearly now. The only thing his wife still wanted from Brazil was *out*.

But Abner Cronin could not bring himself to leave.

His calling was a holy thing, a covenant with God, not something to be cast aside when times got tough. He could no more give up that calling than he could stop breathing or will his heart to stop beating. Neither though could he force any other soul to share the path that had been chosen for him if the calling was not present—even the wife who had promised submission by the biblical standard, till death do them part.

His choice was clear. To serve his Lord, Abner must leave Mercy while she slept and go back to the mission on his own. It might seem cruel, but what else could he do? If they had talked about it through the night, Abner supposed that Mercy would have gone along with him, but that was pointless, when he knew her heart was not committed to the task.

He would have left a note, but where would he find pen and paper in the jungle? They had been snatched out of their home by Braga's thugs then hauled away by Matthew Cooper into another sector of the forest where there was no stationery to be found.

Mercy would understand in time, and Abner prayed that she'd forgive him someday. Come what may, he was bound to follow God's instructions and divest himself of all worldly entanglements that kept him from pursuing that goal.

Now all he had to do was find his way back to the mission through the trackless jungle. In the dark. Alone.

The first step was the hardest, sneaking out of camp without disturbing Mercy, knowing that each yard he traveled took him farther from the life he knew. Abner had never truly been a solitary man, but the word of God told him "but with God all things are possible." He would survive against all odds if God so willed it. And if not, then Abner supposed his death would serve some greater good.

He might turn out to be a martyr yet—but who would know? Or care?

No matter.

Sacrifice was not for show. Scripture admonished true believers to pray in their closets, behind closed doors, rather than sounding trumpets to announce their faith for public adulation. Those who flaunted their religion were condemned by Christ as hell-bound hypocrites.

"'Take therefore no thought for the morrow,'" Abner muttered, as he moved into the jungle. "'For the morrow shall take thought for the things of itself. Sufficient unto the day is the evil thereof.'"

This day had been evil, indeed, but tomorrow was bright with promise. All he had to do was keep the faith, stay strong and forge ahead as he was guided by the Lord, placing his trust in the Twenty-Third Psalm.

Yea, though I walk through the valley of the shadow of death, I will fear no evil: for thou art with me; thy rod and thy staff they comfort me.

And so, Abner wondered, why on earth was he weeping?

BOLAN WAITED UNTIL he was clear of camp to don the night-vision binoculars, turning the jungle an eerie bright green in front of him.

The goggles let him navigate where any hiker unassisted by technology would soon have lost his way. Very useful, also, was the GPS device he had preprogrammed to direct him toward the hardsite where Joaquim Braga maintained his not-so-secret headquarters. The narco-trafficker owned a stately home in Rio de Janeiro—where he wined and dined selected politicians and associates from time to time—and a condo in Brasilia—for those moments when he simply had to wield his power personally in the capital.

Sadly for Braga, Interpol investigations had compelled him to relinquish other homes in Paris and on southern Spain's Costa del Sol, but Braga had discreet hideaways in Zurich and on Grand Bahama, outside Freeport.

None of which would help him when the Executioner came knocking.

Tonight, however, was simply recon, as he'd told the Cronins. Even with the help of satellite photography, Bolan still needed a feel for the place from ground level. A soldier's-eye view of the target. He had no intention of engaging with the enemy beyond what he'd already done that afternoon, but circumstances had a way of changing without prior notice once a battle had been joined. He was prepared for anything as he paced off the miles, watching for predators along the way and drawing closer to his goal with every stride.

At last Bolan stood on the outskirts of the compound. The only lights were those that shone through certain windows or from lamps inside of tents. He heard at least one generator chugging in the night, and Bolan traced its sound to a prefab shed on the camp's southern perimeter. There was no fence encircling the compound—an obstacle to bailing out in the event of unexpected raids. Its absence also meant that Bolan would require no special gear to infiltrate the camp, as long as he could slip past sentries on patrol.

Speaking of which, the guards were out in force. He didn't know what kind of strength was normal for the site, but there were ten men armed with IMBEL MD-2 automatic rifles walking beats around the camp. Each one had a strip of ninety yards or so to cover, marching back and forth, eyes on the forest that pressed close on every side. There was no road to cover, hence no standard motor pool of four-wheeled vehicles. Supplies, Bolan guessed, were either carried in on foot, or—far more likely—flown in via helicopter as required.

And speaking of choppers, intel had it that a major cocaine shipment from Colombia was due tomorrow. If Bolan could meet it, all the better. And if not, well, let the pilot find a smoking ruin when he got there and be forced to turn around and take his cargo home again. In either case, if Bolan had his way, the *marching powder* wasn't getting through this time.

5

Cold Camp, Mato Grosso

Mercy Cronin woke in darkness, startled by the roaring of a jaguar. Had it only been a dream, in fact? She waited, trembling, for the noise to be repeated, but it never came. Instead, she peered around the clearing where she'd drifted off and found herself alone.

"Abner?" She kept her voice pitched low, almost a whisper, worried by the prospect of attracting some nocturnal predator. When there was no reply, she tried more urgently. *"Abner!"*

And still no answer.

Scrambling to her feet, she felt disoriented—a little drowsy from her nap—but she was growing more frightened by the second. Where had Abner gone? He might have left the clearing to relieve himself, but how long could that take?

How long? It struck her that she had no idea when he'd left her side, or even how long she had been asleep. She wore a cheap wristwatch but could not read it in the jungle darkness. Not that it would matter, since she hadn't checked the time before she had dozed off, when Abner had offered to take the first watch. Sometime while she slept, he had not only moved away from her, taking his warmth, but he'd left the clearing altogether.

Leaving her alone. Defenseless.

No! She couldn't make herself believe that Abner would desert her. If he'd stepped into the forest for a moment, answering the call of nature, something could have happened to him. There were snakes, the jaguar that had woken her...

Now Mercy's fear was close to panic. Abner was her husband and her lover, though the loving had admittedly been sparse the past six months or so. They had been married after college, before Mercy ever tried to manage living on her own. She knew the basics, but she couldn't picture life without him.

Reality snapped back at her with that thought, and she almost laughed aloud at her stupidity. Why was she wondering about the details of a normal life alone, when she was stranded in the middle of a jungle wilderness, with no idea of what might happen to her next? It was conceivable that she'd be slaughtered and devoured before sunrise. Problem solved!

Mercy abandoned any pretense of composure, shouting, "Abner! Where are you?"

Her own voice echoed back to her from the surrounding trees, but no one answered. Abner surely would respond if he could hear her, wouldn't think of leaving her in such distress.

Except he had.

The only possible solutions came down to a choice of evils. Either Abner had deserted her or he was lying somewhere in the forest, dead, or incapacitated and unable to respond. It shamed Mercy to realize that she preferred the second choice. That way she'd know he hadn't left her purposely. She could imagine that he had been thinking of her at the end.

And yet...

He didn't want to leave the mission. Even after they

were kidnapped and members of their congregation had been murdered, he had argued for remaining—over Mercy's personal objections—going on as if nothing had happened. Was that dedication? Selfless courage? Or insanity?

If he'd been around to answer questions, Mercy guessed that Abner would have said he was answering God's call. Did that include abandoning his wife to jaguars, snakes and vampire bats? Scripture clearly stated that a husband and wife were *one flesh*. If he'd left her, choosing the Mundurukus over her…

"Damn you, Abner!" Mercy spat into the darkness, then blushed furiously and began the ritual of praying for forgiveness. Abner's sin was no excuse for any lapse on her part.

But the truth was, in that instant, she hated him for leaving her.

There'd been no jaguar mauling, or she would have heard his screams. If he'd been bitten by a snake, however deadly, Abner could have staggered back to camp before collapsing. Quicksand only formed in jungles along riversides or lake shores. Likewise, since they weren't near water, Abner obviously wasn't eaten by a caiman or an anaconda.

He had simply left her to her own devices, without even telling her goodbye.

This time when Mercy cursed him, she felt no regret.

But there was fear, oh, yes. She couldn't get away from that. Her only hope, from this point on, was Matthew Cooper.

And where was he? What if *he* never made it back from his mysterious "recon" and she was left to die alone?

Defeated, Mercy Cronin slumped against the tree where Abner had abandoned her and wept.

Condor Acampamento

IT WAS GETTING late, but Joaquim Braga poured himself another glass of ultra premium *cachaça*.

He needed it tonight, with thirteen of his soldiers dead, two prisoners extracted from their custody and unknown enemies prowling around his turf, perhaps to strike again at any time. Those troubles were the very last thing he needed with Hugo Cardona sleeping in his camp and one thousand kilos of cocaine arriving tomorrow.

He needed that shipment and those which would follow. He needed the heroin, the marijuana and the methamphetamines that Cardona's syndicate could furnish in huge quantities. Beyond the drug consumption in his homeland, there were epic profits to be made in North America and Europe, plus a growing market in South Africa. Why should the Boers and Zulus be denied the pleasure of escape into a land of addled fantasy?

And why should Braga be denied the billions he would earn from them?

Beyond the profits, it was important that he keep Cardona's trust—and most important that his own ferocious reputation be maintained. If it was thought that some competitor could murder Braga's men and get away with it, the jackals would be snapping at his heels forever, forcing him to fight defensive actions on all sides while his business declined into ruin. Vengeance must be swift and merciless, preferably running up a body count double or triple his own recent losses.

First, of course, he had to *find* his enemies, identify them and determine why they felt they could challenge him, today of all days. Understanding might come through interrogation, if his search parties were fortunate enough to bring survivors back tomorrow. Braga made a mental note to tell them he wanted prisoners able to speak. Their questioning could serve a double function—information gathering and entertainment for his troops.

As for the missionaries, Braga assumed they would be found among their rescuers. If the couple believed they could escape from Braga, they were living in a dream world, some pathetic alternate reality. Or were they something more than they appeared to be?

Their extrication from captivity had started Braga thinking. What if they were spies of some kind—for the U.S. Drug Enforcement Administration perhaps—posing as ministers while they collected evidence against him? It would be a strange and cynical approach, but he put nothing past his enemies in Washington.

Not that Braga had any complaint about the Yankee "war on drugs." Without it, Braga's profits would have plummeted. Indeed, if drugs were legalized worldwide, he would become irrelevant, superfluous. God bless America, England and every other nation that had banned narcotics under penalty of law! Braga woke up each morning grateful for their rigid attitudes—and the hypocrisy that kept his product flowing, while it seemed that politicians and police always had their hands out for the next bribe, and the next.

Corruption made the world go round.

Joaquim Braga would not have had it any other way.

Cold Camp, Mato Grosso

BOLAN RETURNED ALONG the green trails lit by his night-vision goggles, satisfied with what he'd learned about the layout and security of Braga's jungle compound. Bolan was looking forward to a short rest—half an hour, say—before the hike to meet Grimaldi and off-load the Cronins at first light. Tomorrow his move against the Braga syndicate would begin in earnest.

Pausing on the outskirts of the clearing where he'd left the missionaries, Bolan noted only one of them in view. Mercy was huddled with her back against a tree, knees drawn up to her chest and forehead resting on her folded arms. From where he stood, he couldn't tell whether she was awake or not, but Abner was not visible.

"Hello, the camp," he called out, watching Mercy jerk upright. At the sight of him emerging from the trees, she bolted to her feet and came halfway to meet him, stopping with ten feet of open ground between them as she started speaking rapidly.

"I was asleep. I didn't see him go. Heard nothing. He was standing watch and then…and then… He's left me!"

Mercy started weeping. Bolan fought the impulse to console her and asked, instead, "How long ago was this?"

"I told you, I was sleeping, and—"

"When did you *notice* he was gone?"

"I'm not sure." Shoulders slumped, she stood defeated in the middle of the clearing. "Hours now, I think. I couldn't read my watch when I woke up."

"What woke you?"

"Well…I thought it was a jaguar, but I can't be sure."

"Not Abner leaving?"

"Definitely not."

Bolan dismissed the jaguar from his mind. Real or imaginary, no big cat had ever killed a person without wreaking bloody, noisy havoc in the process. Neither did he think that Abner Cronin could have gone to take a leak and lost his way. A few steps into darkness would have been sufficient, with the clearing and his wife still plainly visible.

"What did you talk about after I left, before you fell asleep?"

"The mission," Mercy answered. "Abner didn't want to give up on it. He knew I was scared of staying, so…he left."

Bolan accepted that, since Mercy obviously understood her husband better than Bolan ever would. And granting that she was correct, he knew tracking Abner through the dark rain forest was impossible. Whether he made it back to Mercy Mission or got lost somewhere along the way, Abner was well beyond Bolan's reach for the time being.

"You'll find him, won't you?" Mercy asked, pleading.

"I can't follow him tonight," Bolan replied. "I'd miss too many clues along the way, even with these." He raised a hand to tap the goggles folded up against his forehead.

"But—"

"Tomorrow I can try to find his trail. Meanwhile, the best thing you can do is try to get some sleep."

"Oh, no. I couldn't. Abner—"

"Made a conscious choice. You're not responsible. It's not your fault."

"I could have gone with him."

"In which case, I'd be killing time till daylight, then wasting tomorrow hunting both of you. This way, you're safe."

It sounded cold—*was* cold—but Bolan had to keep things in perspective. Rescuing the Cronins once had been an unexpected delay. Having to put his job on hold and doing it all over again was aggravating.

To distract her, Bolan asked, "How's Abner's woodcraft? Can he find his way around the forest fairly well?"

"Oh, yes." She focused, brightened slightly. "He knows all the signs for animals and has a great sense of direction."

"Okay then. That helps. First thing tomorrow, I can hike to the mission. If he's there, I'll bring him back to you."

"But if he doesn't want to leave—"

"I'm not negotiating with him," Bolan said. "He's coming back, like it or not."

"If I go with you—"

"No. You'd only slow me down, and I don't want to referee some big domestic scene with Braga's soldiers hunting us."

She winced at that but nodded, saying, "I suppose you're right. But what if…if he *isn't* at the mission?"

"The State of Mato Grosso covers more than three hundred and forty-eight *thousand* square miles," Bolan answered, "I can't follow Abner all over creation and still do the job I came for. I'll check at the mission, then come back to you. Either way, you'll be leaving soon."

"But not at first light."

"Not with Abner," Bolan said. "You want to take off on the flight that I've scheduled, you leave him behind. Raise a search party later, when I'm finished here—say, day after tomorrow. That's one way to go."

She considered it, then shook her head. "I can't leave him."

"You may have no choice."

"Please look for him!"

"At dawn then. Now go get some rest."

Várzea Grande, Mato Grosso

JACK GRIMALDI LISTENED, standing with his back against the warm flank of the Bell UH-1 Iroquois, scowling. "You're freakin' kidding me. He just gets up and wanders off?"

"He's on a mission," Bolan told him, via sat phone. "You know how that is."

"Uh-huh. But there're missions, and there're *missions*. What, he couldn't wait a couple days to check back on the Indians?"

"It's done," Bolan replied. "I'll try to find him in the morning. If I can't, he stays behind."

"So, what's the ETA look like?"

"Sunrise is close to six o'clock. An hour to the mission, give or take, and then an hour back. Two hours to the LZ, if they can keep up. Say ten o'clock, unless I have to call and push it back."

"Okay," Grimaldi said. "I'll be there."

"Never doubted it," Bolan replied, as he cut the link.

Cold Camp, Mato Grosso

THE SETBACK WASN'T fatal, in and of itself, but Bolan had a schedule to keep. The information he'd received from Stony Man, gleaned from a DEA informant in Colombia, was that the shipment of cocaine inbound for Braga's camp would be arriving at seventeen hundred hours. Bolan's watch ticked off the seconds while he listened to the jungle's nightly chorus.

Nocturnal birds and insects sang throughout the hours of darkness if they weren't disturbed by predators. Amid their calls, Bolan's ears picked out the sounds of a bat swooping to feed on moths, mosquitoes, anything its radar could detect in flight. Outside the clearing where he sat, persistent rustlings in the undergrowth charted the passage of rodents and reptiles, perhaps a Goliath bird-eating spider out trolling for prey. Bolan kept track of all the noises he recognized as normal, staying on alert for their cessation, while he thought through what he had to do over the next few hours.

Sleep was off the table, but he'd rested well before he had dropped into the jungle and was nowhere near the limit of his stamina. He then prioritized his jobs, keeping the deadline for the cocaine drop in mind and working back from there to frame his schedule.

Look for Abner at the mission. If he turned up, retrieve him by any means required. If not, forget him for the moment and evacuate the preacher's wife. From there, get back on track with Braga, taking time to set an ambush at the forest compound and be ready when the drug-filled chopper from Colombia arrived. Rain hell on Braga and his men, his illegal cargo, his transports, everything. The scorched-earth treatment he'd perfected during his one-man war against the Mafia and later in his antiterrorist campaigns.

It sounded simple, when he spelled it out that way. If only life—and death—could be that easy.

Standing watch while Mercy Cronin slept, Bolan ran through what he'd learned about his enemy. Braga was in his mid-forties, a child of Rio de Janeiro's slums who'd clawed his way up from the gutter, literally, to command an outlaw empire. He had started out small, as a thief and street-corner drug peddler, graduating to armed robbery and kidnapping for ransom, then to pandering and human trafficking—the latter enterprise divided between labor contracting for sugarcane plantations and procuring sex slaves for big-city brothels.

Narcotics trafficking had followed as a matter of course—the real bonanza for any would-be gang lord in Latin America. Today, off the record, Braga ranked among the richest twenty-five or thirty people in Brazil.

So he was rich and powerful, with politicians, judges and police commanders on his payroll—none of which meant anything to Bolan. Every mob boss the Executioner had ever toppled from his high roost had the same connections, none of them enough to save them from a skilled, determined warrior.

That, in nearly every case, had turned out to be the weakness of Bolan's enemies. For all their innate ruthlessness and cunning, by the time they'd reached the pinnacle of influence and power, they had begun to count on the protection of the same society they had fastened on, feeding like parasites. Police—the honest ones—played by a set of rules that Bolan recognized but totally ignored. He wasn't taking prisoners, collecting evidence for an indictment or a trial that might drag on for years before a jury deadlocked, only to have the sad charade began again from scratch.

Bolan believed in more direct solutions, in excision of the cancer growing on society. And while he knew that taking out one boss only made way for his replacement—that no victory was ever permanent—Bolan did his part to stem the filthy tide. At home, abroad, it made no difference. The human predator had not been born who was invincible.

Joaquim Braga would die like any other man, if it came to that. His time was running out.

The drug lord simply didn't know it yet.

6

Missão Misericórdia

Abner had made it back alive and more or less unscathed—
except for bruises from a fall along the way. Who could
deny the hand of God at work in a journey through the forest after nightfall, without any instruments to guide him
through the dark and hardly any moonlight? After he'd
evicted several pouting spider monkeys from the mission,
he had knelt to offer up a prayer of thanks, then fell into
a deep and dreamless sleep.

The guilt was waiting for him when he woke, of course.
He had left Mercy on her own—or, more correctly, in the
hands of Matthew Cooper, assuming he returned—and
Abner only hoped she could understand someday. That
she'd forgive him for the choice that had been unavoid-
able. His call from God had simply been an offer he could
not refuse.

Or had he lost his mind?

Several of Abner's so-called friends had offered that
opinion back in Florida, before he'd departed for Brazil.
Without mincing words, two had told him that he was
crazy. Another had thought he was "going overboard on
the religious stuff," while yet another had suggested that
he "needed rest." Until they turned on him, Abner had
not been conscious of the fact that his acquaintances—

though self-identified as Christians—were, in fact, the tools of Lucifer.

He prayed again on waking in the first gray light of dawn, and then he heard his stomach growling. Abner wished he'd taken some of Matt Cooper's MREs before he left the forest camp, but that would have been stealing. Strange how that seemed more repugnant than abandoning his wife of fourteen years. He thought about the seeming contradiction for a moment, then dismissed it with a mental rundown of the Ten Commandments. One banned theft. Another banned the coveting of someone else's wife, but not a word was said about deserting home and family in answer to a holy summons.

Abner found some cans of food in a cupboard, picked one filled with pork and beans for breakfast and prepared to light the mission's small wood-burning stove. The smoke might lure his enemies, but it would also send a signal to the Mundurukus, to let them know that he was back and ready to continue with their spiritual instruction.

Whether they would come or not was something else entirely. Abner trusted God to bring them back, if it turned out to be His will. If not…well, he would certainly feel foolish in that case. His long trek through the jungle would have been for nothing then, if he had no flock to receive his message.

Not *my* message, Abner thought immediately. *God's*.

But if the Mundurukus did not come, then what? If they'd been frightened off by Braga's gunmen and the murder of their kinfolk, what would Abner do? Without his wife, with no link to the outside world, how was he going to proceed?

He would give it time. A few days, at the very least. If no one came to him by then, he'd reconsider staying. He could make it to Cáceres, probably. A long walk to the Rio Paraguai, then follow it downstream to reach the city. From there, a bus ride to the capital, Cuiabá, and he could decide his next move. Try to find out whether Mercy had returned to Florida, gone back to stay with family in Illinois, or if she'd waited somewhere in Brazil to hear from him. Abner had no idea how to begin a search for her among the nation's more than 200 million people, but if he was meant to find her, something would occur to him.

The Lord would help him.

Abner ate his pork and beans. He watched the forest in the vain hope that he'd see at least one Munduruku tribesman peering from the foliage, drawn back to the site where they had shared God's word.

Too soon, he thought. Of course they wouldn't rush back to the mission one day after it was raided and their loved ones were shot. Time was required for mourning rituals, recouping courage.

He'd have to wait and see. But in the meantime, he could fix some of the damage done by Braga's people to the mission.

There was always time to tidy up the house of God.

Cold Camp, Mato Grosso

BOLAN ATE BREAKFAST early, when it was still dark in the forest. He chose an MRE containing maple sausage and hash browns with a slice of bread and blackberry jam. Twelve hundred calories to keep him going through the morning and into early afternoon, and if it wasn't gourmet fare, so what? He wasn't on vacation at the Ritz.

Bolan left Mercy Cronin with instructions to remain exactly where she was, stray no more than a few yards from the camp and keep the clearing in her line of sight regardless. If some prowling forest denizen came by, there was a tree of reasonable size that she could climb, for all the good it would do. This time he left the bolo knife and one of his canteens, then picked up what was left of Abner's trail from his departure in the middle of the night.

It led back toward the mission, no surprise, and when the tracks had played out, Bolan kept going in the same direction. He made no attempt to fathom Abner's thought processes, to determine what would make him leave his wife behind and strike off through the midnight jungle to a site that had been raided once already by his mortal enemies. Religion, when it gripped a mind, sometimes evoked the most bizarre behavior. Only later—sometimes long after the fact—could that behavior be identified as bold or foolish, brilliant or insane.

Motivation held no interest for Bolan this morning. He simply wanted to find Abner Cronin, extract him by any means required and get him on Grimaldi's chopper bound for Várzea Grande. Grimaldi could hand off the missionary couple to consular officials and let the diplomatic red tape stall them for a few days, buying time for Bolan to complete his work against the Braga syndicate. From there on, whether Abner and his wife returned to "save" the Indians or went back to the States meant no more to the Executioner than who won *American Idol*. Once neutralized as obstacles, they were irrelevant.

Monkeys chattered in the trees as Bolan passed beneath them, pausing now and then to check his GPS and verify the course he'd chosen through the forest. Birds screeched, and at a turning in the trail, Bolan surprised a giant peccary some three feet tall that studied him with little piggy eyes before it ambled off into the shadows. Watching out for more of them as he proceeded, Bolan cleared the area without sparking a hog stampede, but he kept the safety off his Steyr AUG as he pressed on.

The jungle wasn't hostile to humanity, per se, as some contended. Personal experience had taught him that the jungle simply didn't care if any given creature lived or died. The wheel of life—and death—kept turning day and night, around the clock, uninterrupted.

In the rain forest, death never took a holiday.

In Medellín, or wherever the cartel's shipment was coming from, he knew the cocaine would be packaged, crated and probably already loaded in the helicopter. Bolan was determined to meet it on arrival.

And he did not plan to let the Cronins keep him from that rendezvous.

Condor Acampamento

JOAQUIM BRAGA WATCHED his men assembling into teams, some of them bleary-eyed from sleep but still on time. They were aware of the penalty for tardiness or any other small infraction of the rules, and each of them had lost friends in yesterday's massacre. They wanted revenge, were thirsty for blood, but Braga knew they would obey his order to return with living prisoners.

If nothing else, they would look forward to the show as he interrogated them.

Hugo Cardona had turned out to watch the hunters leave, although he did not seem to be a morning person. Late nights in the high-priced clubs of Medellín were more his style, Braga supposed. It was a lifestyle Braga, too, enjoyed, during his time in Rio and São Paulo. This was time for work, however.

Time perhaps for war.

Overnight, Braga had hatched a theory—or a strong suspicion. Suppose that *he* was not the target of whoever had attacked his men. What if it was someone who had trailed Cardona to his camp from Medellín? That would explain why Braga, so secure within his jungle fiefdom, suddenly found himself besieged by unknown enemies.

And who would hate Cardona that much? A rival cartel, perhaps: Colombian, Bolivian, Peruvian, pick one. Or could the attackers be government agents? The United States had given up trying to extradite Cardona, but they had other means. Navy SEALs, for example, or the DEA's Special Operations Division. That seemed fitting, since Cardona was charged in the States with killing two DEA agents. Granted, a robot drone attack would be more in keeping with Washington's modern techniques, but who said they couldn't go old school?

Braga reviewed his troops prior to departure. Three teams of twenty men each, all clad in camouflage fatigues and armed with IMBEL rifles furnished by a contact in the Brazilian Army. No one missed the guns or other weapons sold to Braga out of military stores, providing the price was high enough.

His men weren't spit-and-polish perfect, like a normal military unit, but they stood before him at attention, more or less. Braga felt reasonably certain he could trust them to perform the task he'd set—avenging their dead comrades and returning with at least one prisoner who could explain what had prompted yesterday's attack.

Of one thing he felt certain: it could not have been the two preachers. They were nothing, no one, in the global scheme of things. Braga had done his homework and discovered that they were not linked to any major church, sect or denomination in America or Brazil. They had no pope, bishop or ayatollah to concern himself with what became of them. In short they were alone, the very orphans of religion. He could kill them if he liked, and it was probable that no one in the outside world would even notice.

When he had a prisoner in hand—or better, *several* prisoners—Braga would soon sort out the truth. And he would have a good time doing it, impressing both his soldiers and Hugo Cardona with the way in which he punished upstart enemies. Should it turn out that he was right, and his Colombian guest had drawn this trouble to his doorstep, it would give Braga a bit of leverage over Cardona. He did not believe for one split second that Cardona would feel guilty; that was not within his range of recognized emotions. But as businessmen, they could negotiate some kind of compensation, possibly a price cut on his next shipment from Colombia.

He spared the hunters any sort of pep talk, trusting them to nurse their anger and vent it on the enemy when he was placed before them. Roughly half the men in Braga's army had some military service in their background, and while most of those had been dishonorably discharged, they had managed to acquire the basic skills. Beyond that, shooting for his syndicate had toughened them, ensuring they knew exactly when and who to kill.

And he had also taught them who to fear. *O chefe* was their lord and master. He possessed the power of life and death—one profitable and luxurious, the other painful, bloody, absolutely final.

These were men who would not let him down, because their lives depended on success.

Cold Camp, Mato Grosso

MERCY GAVE MATTHEW COOPER ten minutes, all that she could spare under the circumstances, then set out to follow him. If she waited any longer, it was virtually certain that she'd lose him in the forest. Lose herself, in fact, and wander aimlessly until she died from thirst, starvation or the fangs of some cruel predator.

It was embarrassing that she couldn't retrace her steps from where they'd camped last night, back to the mission named for her, but in all fairness it wasn't her fault. She'd been abducted from the mission and was halfway to some other place she'd never seen before—a place where she was likely meant to die—when Cooper had rescued her and Abner, leading them away by other paths to last night's resting spot. And, truth be told, she'd never shared her husband's innate, almost eerie skill at finding his way through new territory.

Some had it, some didn't. Abner had joked with her once, about his days as a Boy Scout hiking and camping in wilderness areas. She'd laughed along with him, enjoying his easy, self-deprecating sense of humor, but in fact she'd been impressed. Mercy could get lost in a shopping mall and then come out to find her car had disappeared, as if by magic. Hours wasted, roaming back and forth through parking lots, until she found the vehicle exactly where she'd left it in the first place.

Not this time.

She wasn't taking any chances with Matt Cooper or her husband's life.

Cooper would be angry if he caught her trailing him, but realistically what could he do? Take her back to their camp, tie her up and then set out all over again? There was a possibility, of course, that he'd abandon Abner—possibly abandon both of them, and go about his strange, unstated business—but she was a fairly decent judge of character and didn't read him as a man who'd be so heartless.

Then again, perhaps she ought to ask the dozen men he'd killed just yesterday.

That had been terrible, and yet she still couldn't help thinking, better them than me.

Was that a sin? Perhaps. She had already asked forgiveness for it, but the attitude hung on.

Trailing the man who'd saved her life back toward the mission, Mercy Cronin was reminded of her feelings when she'd first come to the Amazon with Abner. In those days she had been afraid of everything—the animals, the plants, the weather, terrorists and bandits, even those she'd come to serve among the native tribes. It was a world as alien to her as anything she might have found in outer space and, even trusting God, trusting her husband, had not eased her fears. Time was required to make her feel somewhat at ease, but now she'd been propelled backward in time, reliving all the terrors she had experienced upon arrival in the jungle.

Kidnapped. Nearly murdered. Then abandoned by the man who'd sworn to never leave her side. Now she was following a homicidal stranger through the forest, hoping he would reunite her with her husband.

To what end? She wasn't sure about that, either. If and when she found Abner, would he be pleased to see her, or would he insist that she depart without him? Matthew Cooper had promised to bring Abner out, even if that meant taking him against his will, but what would that accomplish for their marriage? Clearly she and Cooper had different priorities. He was intent on getting rid of obstacles—or witnesses—before he started his mission, while Mercy wanted…what?

In her disoriented state, she couldn't say.

Cooper did not blaze a trail, as such, but rather used a track that had been cleared by animals, perhaps by humans. Had the Mundurukus passed this way on hunting expeditions or while waging war against some rival tribe? Headhunters were another thing Mercy had feared when she and Abner had embarked on their mission, though she had not actually seen a shrunken head so far.

So many things to fear.

But the worst of them was being left alone.

7

Two Miles Northeast of Condor Acampamento

Rain dripped from the brim of Felix Lima's bush hat as his team moved farther away from camp. The rain was warm, and while it plastered camo fabric to his skin, he knew his clothes would dry after a fashion once the rain stopped falling. Soon he would be steaming like some creature in a horror film, and the evaporative action would cool him.

What else could you expect from a *rain forest,* after all?

Leading the search team—and the first team chosen by *o chefe*—was an honor and a privilege Lima had not enjoyed since joining Joaquim Braga's private army. He was not physically leading them, of course, a scout had gone ahead on Lima's orders, but he had command of nineteen men and counted that as some kind of promotion, even if no boost in rank had come along with it.

Once he had proved himself, *then* he would be rewarded handsomely. The fastest team to bring back a living captive for interrogation had been promised a bonus of twenty-five thousand *reals*, about half that amount when converted to U.S. dollars. Hardly a fortune, but the leader's share traditionally came to one-fourth of the total, plenty to raise hell with the next time Lima found himself in Rio de Janeiro.

On the down side, Lima knew he was looking for a team of killers who had slaughtered thirteen of his friends

without a second thought and left all their equipment lying
with their bodies. That was simply showing off, a gesture
indicating that the enemy had no need to collect supplies
after he had killed. It also indicated ruthlessness that Lima
could admire, while fearing it at the same time.

But when the shooting started, as he knew from experience, he would not be afraid.

Lima was somewhat jealous that the second team, led
by Djalma Barbosa, had been sent to check the mission
founded by the preachers. The place might be deserted,
but they had a clear-cut destination to begin with. Lima's
squad and the third one, led by Sérgio Ribeiro, had simply
been ordered to fan out and search the jungle for targets.

Search the *jungle?*

Felix Lima could not quote statistics for the Mato Grosso's size. He had not excelled in geography—or any other
academic subject, for that matter—but he knew the state
was huge. A man could spend his whole life rambling aimlessly through the rain forest and never pass the same point
twice, unless he started walking in a circle accidentally.

That was one error Lima pledged that he would not
commit.

He had a compass and his point man to assist him in
holding a true course, but neither would lead him to success without a healthy dash of luck. His enemies, most
likely, would not be a stationary target waiting for him to
annihilate them. In the rain forest the easiest maneuver—
after getting lost—was eluding trackers. If the hunters
lacked a certain skill, they might be hunted in their own
turn and wiped out.

No problem, Lima thought. He'd been assigned to
Braga's compound for the best part of two years, seeing
the city lights only on short furloughs. He had become
adept at hunting animals and natives, along with the oc-
casional urban adversary whom Braga transported into the

forest for sport. His favorite, so far, had been the Russian mobster who'd been snatched from São Paulo after he had approached some of *o chefe*'s contacts there and offered them a "better deal."

The *russo* was not dealing now.

Lima stepped out of the marching line and watched his soldiers pass, checking for indications of fatigue, distraction, anything that might jeopardize their mission. They were fit and doing well so far—a good thing, since they might be out all day unless they made contact soon.

Contact with whom?

That was the question nagging at Felix Lima's mind as he brought up the rear, marching like a common soldier at the tag end of the column. Not a safe place, necessarily, when danger could appear from anywhere, at any time. Keeping his mind fixed on the bonus he would earn for bagging prisoners, he scanned the woods around him, hoping he would spot a target and dreading it at the same time.

BOLAN CHECKED HIS watch and decided to pick up his pace. He'd covered roughly half the distance from last night's camp to the Cronin mission, spotting signs at several points along the way that could have marked his quarry's passage, though he couldn't actually pin a partial footprint or a broken twig on any individual. How likely was it that Bolan would cross the trail of someone other than the preacher—who'd ditched his wife last night and doubled back to reach the spot where he'd been kidnapped only yesterday?

Bolan had seen religious zeal carried to extremes, and he knew that it affected different minds in different ways. One person might sell everything he owned, donate the cash to charity and spend the rest of his life in solemn meditation. Another might hear voices in his head and launch a personal crusade, attacking synagogues or women's clinics, mosques or military bases. Faith, to Bolan, was a private thing, intensely personal. It could be shared upon request, with someone trusted and well known, but it should never be a weapon.

Grimaldi would be taking off soon. Bolan could have waited until he had Abner Cronin in his hands, then given Grimaldi the signal to begin, but that meant Bolan and his two civilians would be waiting longer at the LZ, while Joaquim Braga's commandos hunted them. Better to have Grimaldi waiting on them. This way, if anything went wrong and Bolan had to abort the pickup, nothing would be wasted but some fuel and a couple hours of Grimaldi's time. Jack wouldn't gripe about it. He had worked with Bolan too many times to think that everything ran smoothly.

Would be nice though, Bolan thought, frowning.

Funny how when you helped some people out of trouble they resented it, ran off on tangents, made things worse, convinced they could do better on their own. It was a part of human nature, he supposed. Cops dreaded being called out to domestic arguments for just that reason: in the middle of a vicious brawl, bloodied combatants were as likely to assault peacekeepers as to welcome aid. His present situation did not rival that, but Abner Cronin's midnight getaway had seriously complicated matters all around.

The sound of voices somewhere up ahead froze Bolan in his tracks. Two speakers, still too far away to make out what they said or even recognize their language. Bolan spent another moment listening, determined that the sounds were coming his way slowly, and he looked around for someplace to conceal himself.

The simple answer: up.

He chose a tree with branches hanging low enough that he could reach them with an easy jump. The Steyr slung across his back, he caught a limb, pulled himself up, then scrambled into thicker foliage. Most people, in his experience, did not look up while they were walking through the wilderness—or on a city street, for that matter—unless some audible disturbance captured their attention. He could wait and watch, see who passed by and then decide what action was required, if any.

Crouching on a tree limb thicker than his torso, Bolan surveyed the ground below. The voices, two of them at least, were silent now, but he could hear someone approaching through the forest undergrowth. Two minutes later, give or take, a solitary man in camouflage passed underneath his perch, armed with an IMBEL rifle, holstered pistol on his right hip, sheathed machete on his left. A scout, perhaps, taking his time and studying the ground in front of him.

Not looking up.

The point man passed, followed by others in a few more minutes. Bolan counted twenty all together, scout included, guessing from the lack of visible insignia on any of their uniforms that they were Braga's men. Their route, if they held to it, would lead them to Bolan's camp from last night, right around the time he would reach the Cronins' mission.

Mercy.

Scowling, Bolan let the last soldier in line pass by, gave him a lead, then scrambled down to follow.

MERCY CRONIN HEARD the voices too and nearly panicked. In a harried heartbeat, she considered her three options: turn and flee; rush forward, trying to catch up with Cooper; or find a place to hide. The first two both involved considerable noise, since moving quietly required deliberation and a concentration that was almost physically exhausting. Thus her choice was made—but where could she conceal herself?

She could try to climb a tree, but she was only five feet

four inches tall, and the lowest limb on any major tree surrounding her was a minimum ten feet off the ground. Even
leaping, with arms raised high, it was apparent that she
could not reach a sturdy limb *and* pull herself into a decent hiding place. The men approaching—she recognized
male voices, although not what they were saying—would
arrive and find her dangling from the branch, defenseless.

Somewhere on the ground then, but…

Turning to scan the undergrowth, Mercy spied a fallen
tree she had ignored in passing, focused as she was on
trailing Matthew Cooper. Half hidden by a screen of waist-
high ferns, it was a good-size tree—or log, now, she supposed—with branches on its upper side still basically
intact. Mercy thought she could hide behind it, if the hunters did not look too closely. Better yet, as she approached
the log, she saw that it was hollowed out at one end, where
the inner wood had rotted. She could not see all the way
through to the other end, but if the fallen tree had room
enough for her to crawl inside, she would be safer still.

Unless the log was occupied.

She thought about what might be living in the dead
tree's inner darkness. Insects, certainly, which would attract the predators of their world: lizards, spiders, scorpions and centipedes that grew up to a foot in length with
jaws that could inflict a painful, toxic bite. A bushmas-
ter or coral snake might even use the dead tree as a nest.
The thought of being wedged in darkness while a host of
creatures that she couldn't even see crept over her, biting
and stinging, turned her stomach. Mercy knew she could
not force herself to crawl inside the log, but if she hid behind it, maybe even held her breath until the human danger passed, she might be safe.

She moved around the log, inspecting its far side for
snakes and nests of stinging ants before she lay down close
to it, facing in the direction she'd been headed when she

heard the voices, pressed against the log's rough bark from shoulder to ankle. Trembling, tearful, she came close to cursing Abner once more, then realized this part of her predicament was her own doing. If she'd stayed in camp as Cooper had told her, she wouldn't be in this position, waiting to find out if she would be kidnapped again or simply shot on sight.

And where *was* Cooper? It seemed the men approaching her had passed the point where Cooper should be, well out ahead of her, so that she barely glimpsed him at intervals as Mercy followed him. There'd been no shooting, so she reckoned they must not have seen him. Had he found a place to hide, as well? No doubt, he would be more adept at it than she was, safer in whatever cover he had found.

If the approaching men saw Mercy, if they started to attack or kidnap her, would Cooper step in to rescue her a second time? Or would he be so furious that she'd disobeyed him, followed him against his orders, that he'd leave her to her fate?

Turning her face away, pressing her cheek into the soft soil of the forest floor, Mercy lay still and waited to find out if this would be her final day on earth.

FELIX LIMA THOUGHT his men were making decent time. They'd all been out on various patrols before and knew the jungle fairly well—if not this part of it, precisely, then the animals and plants, the soil, the weather. All of them were city boys to start with, but they had adapted to the Mato Grosso when it was required of them, because *o chefe* willed it so.

Lima had tired of bringing up the rear and granted a brief rest stop, as much for his own dignity as any real concern about the men. It might be awkward if he had to jog the full length of the column to regain his place in front and damned embarrassing if he fell down along the way.

They might not laugh at him immediately—most of them were too intelligent to make that serious mistake—but they would not forget it, either. It was better to pretend he cared how they were doing, whether they were tired, and thus forestall humiliation for himself.

After the rest stop—ten short minutes during which the men swigged whatever it was they carried in their canteens—the march resumed with Lima at its head. The scout was still farther in front to watch for traps—or spring them, if his luck ran out. It would reflect poorly on Lima if he lost a man, but sacrificing one to save the rest did not strike Lima as a problem. Most particularly when one of the lives he saved turned out to be his own.

Alas, the rigors of command.

Lima was getting restless as they slogged along, wishing that something would occur to break the monotony. He loathed the thought of going back to Braga empty-handed—a disgrace if the competing teams bagged captives—but it would be barely tolerable if they all returned with nothing to show for their efforts. Even if he caught one of the natives the missionaries had been working with, trying to educate, it would be *something*. Braga might be able to elicit some response to questioning. Find out if enemies had visited the mission, for example, to plan a war against the syndicate.

That seemed unlikely, granted. Why would anyone discuss such business in the midst of savages? But then again, why scheme with do-gooders in the first place, unless they were something more than simple preachers. Spies, perhaps, disguised as ministers to make themselves seem innocent and harmless.

Possible, thought Lima. The authorities used underhanded tricks routinely, while a rival drug cartel might well decide to gather on-the-scene intelligence before it made a move. Only interrogation of the so-called preachers and the men who'd rescued them would bare the truth of what had happened yesterday.

Lima was packing two canteens, one filled with water, the other with *cachaça* for emergencies. Or for a time like this, when he was feeling weary and required a pick-me-up. He had raised the second canteen to his lips when someone called out from the rear ranks of the column.

"Onde é Thiago?"

Lima turned and looked back along the line of soldiers, frowning to himself. Where *was* Thiago? He'd been bringing up the rear, but now there was no sign of him. How could he possibly get separated from the team so soon after a rest stop?

Lima halted the column. He hurried back along the trail, replacing his canteen before he had a chance to taste the liquor, easing his rifle off its shoulder sling. Reaching the man who now was last in line, a soldier named Aluizio, he demanded, "When did you last see him?"

Aluizio shrugged. "I heard a noise like coughing, then looked back, and he was gone."

Lima called out, "Thiago! Answer me! Where are you?"

But Thiago did not reply. Instead, a spider monkey cackled somewhere in the canopy above them, while a blue macaw whistled derisively.

"Thiago! Say something!"

And again the missing man said nothing.

"Merda! We must find him," Lima told the soldiers who had drifted back, surrounding him. "You, you and you. Fan out and search for him. The rest, stay here. Don't move a step unless I order it."

Reluctantly the searchers started back along the ground they'd covered moments earlier, calling Thiago's name and getting no response.

THIAGO WASN'T ANSWERING because a Parabellum slug from Bolan's SIG Sauer P226 had clipped his spinal cord between the styloid process and the first cervical vertebrae, immediately snuffing out his life. The shot was nearly silent—or no louder than the muffled coughing sound Aluizio had noted as he hiked along the narrow trail. Before he'd turned around to look, Bolan had hauled the corpse aside and was already moving toward a new position in relation to the line of nineteen riflemen.

He had started with a twenty-round magazine in the P226, plus one round in the chamber. Firing one still left him with enough to take down the rest of the team, but Bolan knew the odds were against him on that. Still he'd do what he could before all hell broke loose in the jungle and he was compelled to go hard with the Steyr AUG.

Three men were coming back to find the one he'd dropped already, calling out what Bolan took to be the dead man's name and shouting other things he couldn't translate. Bolan waited in the shadows, let the nearest of them pass within arm's reach, and kissed him with a Parabellum round behind one ear. The soldier dropped, not silently, and as his comrades turned, the SIG spat two more rounds from twenty feet.

Four down.

Back on the line, their leader understood that something was amiss and badly so. He cried out, "Aluizio! Octávio! Luis! What's happening? Answer me, damn it!"

Bolan was off and moving to the left side of the column, gliding like a shadow through the forest as sixteen survivors huddled closer to their shouting leader. This was crunch time, when he knew the balance could be tipped against him instantly by any small mistake. When he'd flanked them, Bolan moved in closer—steadying the SIG in a two-handed grip—and started rapid-firing through the foliage.

Five, six, seven down, blood spouting from their shattered skulls. Some of the others—sprayed with blood and brains, or jostled as their dying comrades slumped against them—turned, aghast, and raised their weapons, searching for a target.

Eight, nine down, then Bolan ducked and rolled away. One of the soldiers crumpling in a heap triggered a burst of auto fire before his rifle kicked free of his grasp. Those bullets ripped through number ten, and then the rest were diving, scattering to save themselves.

Too late.

While bursts of 5.56 mm NATO rounds peppered the trees and shrubbery above him, Bolan wriggled on his stomach to a new position, fired his pistol from a worm's-eye view and picked off two more riflemen. Ten rounds still remained in his pistol as he crawled beneath the wild fire poured into the trees by survivors who had no idea how many enemies they faced or where the killing fire was coming from.

Thirteen and fourteen down, their bodies still thrashing on the forest floor. A mere half-dozen men remained, abandoning any pretense of discipline as they attempted to escape. Their leader held his ground, kneeling and firing short bursts randomly into the shadows that surrounded him, the others running for their lives.

A Parabellum round from Bolan's SIG punched through the leader's left eye, slammed him over on his back, and he was done. The Executioner was up and running then, chasing a pair of shooters who had broken to his right and back along the trail they'd followed to the ambush site. If either of them heard him coming, they were too intent on flight to turn and fire. The SIG coughed twice more and they fell, spines severed, dead or dying by the time they hit the deck facedown.

What about the other three? Bolan turned back, hunting, and found one cursing furiously as he fought to clear a jammed shell from his weapon's chamber. Bolan shot him on the run, passed by before the body toppled over, searching for the other two.

Scorched earth. No prisoners.

8

Mercy Cronin panicked at the first explosive sounds of gunfire, bolting from her hiding place and running off into the forest away from the trail she'd been following since daybreak. She suppressed an urge to scream, knowing it might prove fatal, but in every other sense her fear was absolute, erasing any thought beyond escape.

And within moments she was lost.

The gunfire, while it lasted, did provide a point of reference, but she was not about to head in *that* direction, back toward what she thought must be another massacre in progress. Matthew Cooper was killing more of Braga's men, or *someone's* men. She understood instinctively that so much shooting would not be required to slay a single man, but must instead mean that the party she'd heard tramping through the rain forest was fighting for its life.

And losing, she decided, when the shooting halted.

She stopped, as well, considering the implications of that sudden silence. Cooper, she thought, had probably destroyed another raiding party sent into the jungle by her enemy. It now occurred to her that she had panicked prematurely, run away for no good reason. Naturally, she couldn't have known that, and she still might be mistaken, but what she had seen of Cooper so far convinced her that he'd probably survived and triumphed with this second battle in as many days.

I should go back, she thought, turning in the direction she had fled from, wondering if she could still catch up to Cooper.

But *was* she facing in the right direction? Every tree around her looked the same to Mercy, and no matter how she searched the undergrowth, she found no signs to re-assure her. In the movies, trackers always found a bro-ken twig or flattened leaf, a fresh scratch on a tree trunk, stones displaced by footsteps—*something* that allowed them to keep going in the right direction, following their prey. As far as she could tell, the ferns and shrubbery sur-rounding her appeared pristine, revealing no hint that she had crashed through them seconds earlier.

"Damn it!" she hissed, and in her agitation failed to ask forgiveness.

Getting lost was something Mercy understood. This would not be the first time she had gone astray, even on short walks from the mission to retrieve firewood or water, but she found it inconceivable that she could lose her own trail instantly, mere seconds after she had stopped running from the sounds of combat.

Sounds.

She strained her ears, hoping there'd be another shot, perhaps a coup de grâce, to help her orient herself, but all she heard were normal forest noises coming back after the shocking interruption of gunfire. After a long five min-utes, when she realized that it was hopeless, tears brimmed in her eyes.

And she blamed Abner.

If he'd been a proper husband, if he hadn't left her in the middle of the night, she wouldn't be in this position. She had no idea how to find the mission, Matthew Cooper or the camp where she'd spent last night. It struck Mercy that she could wander through the vast and trackless jungle till she died from one cause or another, and no one would ever know what had become of her.

Likely no one would care.

She started walking, hoped that she was heading in the general direction she had come from, though she saw nothing familiar along the way. Blind panic had prevented her from memorizing any landmarks as she ran, not that the jungle offered much of anything in that regard to start with. There were no great peaks or boulders, she had crossed no rivers, seen no trees distinctly scarred by lightning.

Nothing.

As she walked, Mercy began to ruminate on ways of dying in the jungle. Dehydration seemed unlikely in a rain forest, although she recognized the dangers of consuming water that had not been boiled. Starvation, on the other hand, was altogether possible. Before leaving Miami, she had read a book about surviving in the wild on nuts and roots, that kind of thing, but she remembered next to nothing of it. As for catching game, she knew that was a hopeless fantasy.

How long could a reasonably healthy person survive without food? A week? Two weeks? Mercy decided that it hardly mattered, since she'd likely die from some other cause before then. Snakebite. An accident that left her physically disabled and defenseless.

Sending up a silent prayer for guidance, she slogged on.

SÉRGIO RIBEIRO HEARD the crackling sounds of gunfire, guessing he was less than a mile southeast of the battle site. Fixing its direction in his mind, he stopped his column, the third squad, called the point man back, and pondered what he ought to do.

Oswaldo Ramos had instructed him to search the forest for the prisoners who had escaped and for the men who'd helped them, killing a dozen of his comrades in the

process. Ribeiro had been pointed southeast of Condor
Acampamento, but should he ignore the noise of battle as
if nothing had occurred?

Soldiers who served *o chefe* walked a fine line between
following their orders to the letter and displaying personal
initiative. Whichever path he chose, Ribeiro knew there
would be pitfalls. Leave the trail he'd been assigned to,
and he risked returning to the compound empty-handed.
Or, if he ignored the obvious—that someone else's team
had seemingly engaged the enemy—he might be branded
a coward. Either course of action might incur his master's
wrath, depending on the ultimate result.

Ribeiro made his choice. If he did not investigate the
shooting, if another of the teams was wiped out when
he could have offered some assistance, the full weight of
Braga's punishment would no doubt fall on him. Con-
versely, if he reached the scene in time to help—or even
to confirm a victory against their unknown enemies—Ribeiro might share in the glory of the victors. Come what
may, once he determined what was happening, he could
proceed as ordered on the course selected for him and
complete his jungle search.

And so his column struck off toward the killing site,
where silence had descended on the forest once again. Ribeiro didn't know what he should make of that, if anything,
but he could not help speculating, playing out scenarios as
he followed his point man, breaking trail.

He had no doubt that one of the competing teams dispatched by Ramos had encountered opposition. That said,
once the shooting stopped, it meant that they had either
overcome their enemies or had themselves been slain. If it
was victory, and living adversaries had been captured, then
the mission was complete. If not…well, that was where
Ribeiro's problem lay.

If he pressed on to find Barbosa's team or Lima's column massacred, what then? His men could not drag twenty corpses through the forest, back to Braga's compound. Save their weapons and equipment, certainly, but dead meat in the jungle decomposed in record time, drew swarms of biting flies and generally made life miserable for the living. Neither had they come equipped with tools for a mass burial, assuming they could dig and hack their way through tree roots using anything available in camp.

So, if he found another of the teams wiped out, the best that Ribeiro could offer *o chefe* was a stack of dead men's guns and more bad news. Hardly the recipe for a reward.

Or he could try to make the best of it and press on from the slaughter cite, pick up the trail of the assassins and destroy them, hoping one or two would fall into his hands while they were still alive and fit for questioning. Avenge his fellow soldiers *and* bring home a prize for Braga.

Better.

In the rain forest, it was difficult to track the source of a sound. Depending on the echo factor, wind and humidity, a calling bird might be somewhere directly overhead or half a mile away. Gunshots, particularly, were deceptive, and a lone report could rarely be traced back to any source. This time, however, there'd been many shots, and Sérgio Ribeiro felt a fair degree of confidence that he was headed in the right direction. As to distance, though...

They had been marching for a half hour when the point man raised a shout, then doubled back to join the team. Ribeiro stood with rifle cocked and ready, watching as the man emerged from the shadows, noting that he did not come alone. Stumbling along beside him, clutched by one wrist, was a woman.

Ribeiro recognized the Anglo missionary's wife and finally allowed himself a smile.

MACK BOLAN OVERTOOK the last two members of the Braga search team one by one, tracking the noise they made while fleeing through the jungle. They'd have had a better chance sticking together, maybe, but the sight of their companions dropping from Bolan's silenced SIG rounds had panicked the survivors who were quick enough to bolt in different directions.

More time wasted, but he couldn't let them get back to the compound and report.

With that in mind, his first priority was taking out the one who'd picked the most direct path back to Braga's camp, churning along the trail his team had followed to the ambush site. There was no real finesse involved, just hot pursuit. The runner must have thought he was clear, because he never looked back once and didn't leave the trail to look for cover when he could have. With his own pulse pounding in his ears, his rasping breath, he likely never heard the Executioner behind him, running hard to close the gap.

Then, on a straightaway, Bolan had stopped and let a bullet close it for him, slamming home between the fleeing gunman's shoulder blades around heart level, damage to the spine immediate and crippling. Bolan didn't check the kill, knowing that even if he'd somehow missed the shooter's heart and his aorta, Braga's man was going nowhere. He'd bleed out in minutes.

He was done.

From there, Bolan had doubled back to find the other one, trusting forest sounds and silences to guide him. Where a human passed in haste, the birdcalls ceased and monkeys either shrieked or scattered. In this forest realm, he knew that nothing but a jaguar or a tapir matched a man in terms of size. Jaguars were silent on the hunt, and tapirs spent most of their time near water, so a noisy thrashing in the undergrowth close by the recent skirmish site meant a human running for his life, desperate to escape the kill zone.

The last guy made it interesting. He kept on running long enough for Bolan to pick up his trail and gain some ground, but then he stopped. The only one of the two who'd used his head, although he'd left it pretty late. In his defense, he hadn't known he faced only one man, or which of the escaping soldiers the Executioner would follow first. The instinct for a long head start was logical enough, but he'd been too noisy in the process to escape notice completely.

Now it was a stalking game. Bolan had hunted silently, waiting for men in situations such as this before, on turf distinctly similar. He knew the signs to look for, could distinguish the aroma of a sweating human body from a forest quadruped that's rolled in mud or had a shower in the rain. He knew a partial footprint when he saw one, and a scuff left by a boot on stone or gnarled tree roots. It wasn't something you learned from books, but rather through experience, surviving in the wild when other humans meant to kill you and the only method of survival was to kill them first.

He found the last man huddled in the shadow of a giant tree, watching a narrow path he'd forged to get there. Bolan didn't try to frighten him, just came around behind him with the SIG and ended it, a head shot fired from ten feet out that put the final member of the search team down and out.

He was definitely running late now, losing time he could not afford.

Scowling, he checked the GPS, confirmed his course, and struck off for the mission once again.

Várzea Grande, Mato Grosso

JACK GRIMALDI LIFTED off in his Bell UH-1 Iroquois right on
schedule. He had agreed to be on station at the LZ by ten,
an hour's flight from Marechal Rondon International Airport. Bolan should be waiting with the people he wanted
Grimaldi to clear out of the way, then Bolan could proceed
with spoiling Joaquim Braga's day.

Grimaldi had already touched base with the U.S. consulate in São Paulo, warning an attaché there that two
Americans had met with trouble in the Mato Grosso and
would need assistance—or some counseling about their
options for the future. Names would have to wait, and
Grimaldi was sketchy on the details. He couldn't tell the
lady he had spoken to exactly how he'd met the folks he
would be bringing in or what the nature of his business
was. When pressed, he'd cited national security and re-
ferred her to a cut-out number that would put her through
to Stony Man but still remain untraceable. Whatever happened to the jungle stragglers after that was none of his
concern.

None of Bolan's, either, once the field of fire was clear.

Grimaldi's second flight over the jungle in as many days
was not relaxing. Even though he felt his best when flying, always had since learning in the army long ago, there
were too many variables this time for his mind to be at
ease. Bolan was off script with the current rescue mission,
had already clashed with Braga's men then disengaged to
babysit the hostages. That wouldn't stop the narco-trafficker from hunting Bolan, putting the master plan at risk.

Grimaldi knew the basics: Braga in his old friend's
crosshairs, with a major cocaine shipment flying in this
afternoon. The strike was meant to be coordinated, taking out the cargo *and* the drug lord's army in a single
stroke. No minor operation, that. It was a challenge even

for a fighting man of Bolan's capability, but the distraction forced upon him by a pair of innocent civilians jeopardized the timeline.

Which meant jeopardizing Bolan's life.

So, what else was new? Grimaldi had backed Bolan's play on dozens of desperate missions, each with the potential for ending Bolan's life. He'd never seen the big guy hesitate to help someone in need, even when doing so increased the odds against him. In another time and place, another war, that tendency had seen him nicknamed Sergeant Mercy, even while he had earned his designation as the Executioner.

Split personality? Not even close.

Bolan had always seemed to know exactly what he wanted out of life. He might not have welcomed it—back in the days when he'd lost his family to tragedy, embarked on the path to vengeance and then to a more noble pursuit—but once committed to the fight, he had not wavered.

Grimaldi called him a hero, the old-fashioned definition of that term, before it was applied to anyone who ever donned a uniform, whether or not they'd been tried by fire. These days, it seemed some people thought they were heroic just for showing up, taking an oath, then disappearing for the duration of a stint that cost them nothing but a little time. Better than sitting home and doing nothing, granted, but a *hero,* to Grimaldi, was a guy who charged the barricades, who threw himself on a grenade to save his friends.

A guy who risked it all, time and again, because *he could.*

Such men—and women, too, damn right—weren't those who had joined the service or a law enforcement agency because they liked the uniform or craved some measure of authority over their fellow citizens. They didn't do it for political advantage down the road, or for a pension that

was guaranteed by Uncle Sam. They acted from a sense
of honor, answering the call of duty, and they fought until
they dropped.

And all of them, eventually, fell.

But not today. Not if Grimaldi could prevent it. Whether
he was getting stragglers out of Bolan's way or roaring in
with rockets and a pair of miniguns ablaze, he had the big
guy's back. Today and in the future, till he finally went
down in flames himself.

Missão Misericórdia

WEARY FROM repairing the mission, Abner kept working
nonetheless. He had not come so far against all odds simply to lie down on his bunk and rest. There would be
time enough for that when he'd put God's house in perfect order—well, as perfect as he could, under the circumstances—and then he must locate the Mundurukus.
If and when he found them, he would beg them to forgive
him for the losses they had suffered, through his failure
to protect them.

If forgiveness was beyond them, at least Abner would
have tried.

He thought about Mercy, wondering if she was safe, and
that thought in its turn embarrassed him. He'd lost—no,
given up—the right to be concerned about her when he'd
left in the middle of the night and struck off on his own.
Most of his former friends in Florida would scorn him for
it, blaming it on ego, but they didn't understand the depth
of his commitment to the Lord. A man who had the calling must be ready to surrender everything that tied him to
the world, whether family, acquaintances or earthly goods
might prevent him from following God's path.

That path had led him here, and now all he could do
was make the best of it.

Or die in the attempt.

Abner felt grubby, filthy, after all that he'd been through since yesterday. The kidnapping and rescue, followed by his night hike through the rain forest, and all the work he'd done to put the mission back in shape after the raid. He craved a bath, which meant another short hike to the nearby river where they—*he*, now—drew the mission's water. Satisfied that he could spare the time, and that the wash-up might improve his spirits when he went to find the Mundurukus, Abner found a bar of soap, one of their threadbare towels and left the mission walking southward toward the river.

He had never heard the natives call this river by a name. Perhaps it wasn't large enough to rate one. Twenty feet or so in width, no more than chest-high at the deepest point he'd found so far, it wasn't much as jungle rivers went. Thanks to the constant rain, of course, it never came up short of water. Boiling was required to make that water potable, but it was fine for bathing if he didn't swallow any in the process.

What he had to watch for near the river were the jungle denizens who came to drink from it and those inhabiting its waters. Piranhas were a danger, as were caimans and electric eels—which, in fact, were not eels at all, but a species of air-breathing fish that could paralyze prey with a charge of some six hundred volts. Anacondas appeared in the river from time to time, but Abner worried more about the toothpick fish, or *candiru,* said to invade the urethras of nude swimmers.

Reasons enough to remain near the shore and indulge in a spit bath of sorts, taking care not to wade out too far. It was better than nothing, and this was the jungle. No one he was likely to meet would expect Abner to look or smell as if he'd just emerged from Bath & Body Works.

He stripped down on the riverbank, folded his towel

over his clothes and took the soap with him as he waded knee-deep into the rushing stream. Crouching, he had begun to lather up his lower body when a voice called out behind him, "Hey, *filho de puta!* Are you cleaning up for us?"

WHEN BOLAN GOT to Mercy Mission, there was no one home. He looked around the place, calling for Abner Cronin and getting no response. The mission had sustained some damage in the raid by Braga's soldiers, but it wasn't terrible. More to the point, Bolan saw that someone had returned and tried to tidy up. The wood stove, freshly stocked and smoking, verified that assessment, as did traces of a recent meal—canned beans, he thought—remaining in a pot and bowl, as yet unwashed. Since there was only one bowl, with a single spoon, he didn't need a CSI report to tell him Abner Cronin had come home.

But where was he?

Bolan thought it over, conscious of the time he was losing in the process, and decided that the missionary must have gone to run some errand. With no settlements nearby, what was the logical conclusion? Further clean-up chores, which might require fresh water.

Bolan looked around for tracks and found the bare earth of the mission beaten flat by human feet. No great surprise. Abner and Mercy had been here for two years, give or take, serving a native congregation that presumably traveled on foot. Three minutes into circling the perimeter, he found a path that led southward, wide enough for two people to pass if they were slim and rubbing shoulders.

Bolan followed it for something like a hundred yards and came out on a river's bank. That solved the water problem, but there was no sign of Abner Cronin on the shore or in the river. He was close to turning back when something caught his eye, just at the water's edge. A hint of faded color, rippling with the gentle current.

Moving closer, Bolan recognized a well-worn towel half in the water, half on shore. Beside it lay a bar of soap, some lather still adhering to its surface.

Bath time, maybe, but the bather had departed. He had either dressed before he left, or tossed his clothes into the river's flow and let them go downstream. That made no sense to Bolan, and he didn't think Abner would lather up his bar of soap before undressing, either. The conclusion: he'd been interrupted, not by something that had snatched him from the river while he bathed, but by some*one,* who'd come upon him from the landward side and gave him time to clothe himself before they left together.

More of Braga's men?

A further search along the riverbank confirmed it to his satisfaction. Footprints of a hunting party, call it twenty strong, approached the spot where Abner left his soap and towel, then retreated in the general direction of the drug lord's forest compound. After ditching Bolan and his wife last night, the preacher had been caught again.

Which ruined everything.

Grimaldi would soon be prepping the helicopter, doing his preflight checks, and Bolan had no time to search for Abner, rescue him once more, double back for Mercy and proceed with them to either of the LZs in time to meet with Grimaldi. Bolan would have to scrub the airlift yet a second time, then see what he could do for the infuriating preacher. Bolan would try to save that life if he could manage it—or Mercy's, at the very least—and still keep his appointment with the cocaine shipment flying in this very afternoon.

Tick-tock.

He frankly wasn't sure if Abner rated any further effort, but that wasn't Bolan's call. He still felt duty bound to try. And after that?

Hell, you could only save a man so many times, if he was bent on suicide. Beyond a certain point, it was both futile and ridiculous.

But he would give it one more try.

The trail was plain for him to follow, Braga's people making no attempt to hide their tracks. They had their prize and would be hurrying back home to show it off.

Unless the Executioner could stop them first.

9

Northwest of Cáceres

Jack Grimaldi took the sat phone call at an altitude of fifteen thousand feet above the jungle canopy. Bad news again—the pickup scrubbed—but his frustration barely registered beside his concern for Bolan. When the Executioner flipped into Sergeant Mercy mode, he never actually lost his focus on the mission, but he rearranged priorities within a heartbeat, veering off on tangents that Grimaldi sometimes feared were detrimental to the greater good.

Not that he'd ever bitched about it, much less challenged Bolan's choices. This was Mack for-God's-sake *Bolan,* after all. He'd never scrubbed a mission and had absolutely never dropped the ball on any job he undertook. But it was tough on those around the battle zone's periphery, watching him deviate from course to save a damsel in distress or keep some clumsy bystander from checking out ahead of schedule.

That was part of what made Bolan who he was, for sure—but damn, it could be nerve-racking.

Grimaldi didn't mind the flying back and forth—the cost of fuel would be reimbursed from Stony Man—but when some yokel he had never met put Bolan's life in danger on a stupid whim, it pissed Grimaldi off. The rambling preacher should have thanked Whomever he believed in that (a) he had Bolan on the ground trying to help him, and (b) he wasn't anywhere within arm's reach of Grimaldi right now.

Sometimes Grimaldi thought, a nice brisk beating did a world of good for idiots.

So he was heading back to Várzea Grande and Marechal Rondon International, his morning wasted on a false alarm. On touchdown he'd refuel the Huey and keep it ready, hang out at the airport for the call to come and try again. Next time perhaps he could complete the babysitting run and settle down to business for the main event.

He'd have to call the consulate, as well, alert them to the fresh delay. That wouldn't win him any friends, but Grimaldi had already established his ability to pull rank with the Feds in Washington, and he could always flex those guns again if necessary. He got no kick from spoiling anybody's day—except the bad guys; he loved that part— but right was right, and red tape wouldn't strangle Bolan on Grimaldi's watch, if he had anything to say about it.

Somewhere down below the forest canopy, his best friend in the world was risking everything for people who, it seemed, were cavalier about their lives and any danger they posed to others. Grimaldi, given the choice, might have allowed them to go skipping off a cliff, but that call wasn't his.

Lucky for them.

He hoped that someday, somehow, they would recognize the gift they'd been given when their troubled path crossed Bolan's in the wilderness, where no one else could help them and the only other folks around wanted them dead.

If not, given the chance, he would be glad to spell it out for them in no uncertain terms.

DJALMA BARBOSA WAS a happy man. He'd found one of the missionaries who'd escaped the day before. The woman wasn't with him, but the preacher had explained that. He had left her somewhere in the jungle, stupid wretch that he was, and had gone back to the mission by himself.

To keep her safe, he said, which made Barbosa think he was crazy. When was any Anglo woman safer in the jungle, on her own, than with a man?

Maybe that Sheena from the movies. Now the missionary's poor wife, on the other hand…well, she could easily be dead by now. And what did that make him? A little man who had indulged himself and chased his superstition while the woman he had sworn to love and cherish died alone and terrified.

In fact, Barbosa didn't care what Mrs. Missionary might have suffered; that was all beside the point. He simply hated cowards and was always glad to see one punished, tormented, humiliated.

On the other hand, he owed the preacher a debt of gratitude for being such an idiot that he let Barbosa capture him, thereby causing Barbosa to earn *o chefe*'s praise and possibly some lucrative reward. Barbosa could explain the missing woman. Leaving her behind was just the sort of thing one might expect from a religious lunatic. With them, it was all "God this" and "God that," while people who depended on them got the short end of the stick.

Barbosa could not picture any of *o chefe*'s enemies lifting a finger for a piece of garbage like his prisoner. It must have been coincidence, he thought, that Mr. Missionary and his wife had happened to be along when the annihilators had struck Aranha's squad. It perplexed him, granted, that whoever did the killing had allowed two witnesses to live, but that was not Barbosa's problem. He'd been sent to search the mission and had bagged one of the runaways. Job done.

But as they marched back toward the compound, he remained alert, on edge. The bastards who had taken out

Aranha and his men were still in the vicinity, no doubt preparing for their next move. And from the far-off gunfire that Barbosa had heard earlier, perhaps that move was underway. If so, the blow had fallen on somebody else, and he was not in a position to assist them.

Just as well.

If there was fighting to be done, he hoped it would be at the compound, with the rest of Braga's soldiers present and the camp's full arsenal available. Barbosa didn't relish being ambushed in the forest, possibly outnumbered and outgunned by enemies he couldn't even see. That kind of combat was uncivilized, something for savages. Barbosa liked an urban jungle best, and failing that, a fortified position he could defend.

For now, he was a winner in the game, returning with his prize. *O chefe* would be pleased, and the Colombian who'd come to visit them should also be impressed. The fact that he was bringing home a sort of human sacrifice did not disturb Barbosa in the least.

It made him smile.

THE TRAIL WAS not particularly hard to follow. Braga's men were in a hurry, it appeared, and not concerned with covering their tracks. Bolan couldn't be sure what kind of lead they had on him, but simple logic told him that the hunters would have started their patrols at daybreak, more or less. Knowing the distance from their base camp to the mission, Bolan calculated that they must have captured Abner Cronin sometime in the past hour to ninety minutes.

He had a chance to overtake them yet.

Braga would have recruited city boys, much like himself. Assuming some—or most—of them had military training in their backgrounds, they could navigate through the rain forest, but they weren't a part of it. All things being equal, twenty-odd guerrillas, with a frightened captive in

their midst, would move more slowly than a single seasoned jungle fighter following behind them. If he caught
the squad before it reached the compound, Bolan thought
he had a decent chance of pulling Abner out a second time.

Decent, but far from guaranteed.

Once the battle had been joined, he knew that anything could happen. Telling someone to expect the unexpected was an oxymoron, but it fit the grim reality of
combat. Anything that *could* go wrong, most likely *would*
go wrong. The best of weapons sometimes jammed when
they were needed most. Vehicles stalled and died. The
weather turned and washed away your best-laid plans. A
sentry sneezed and wound up dead because of it.

Bolan was a master at adapting, going with the flow,
but he could not predict the future. Couldn't have fore-
seen that Abner would desert his wife and run off to be
snatched by Braga's soldiers for a second time. Had no
idea if one more rescue bid would spell the end of Bolan,
his mission, everything.

But he was bound to try.

Bolan was simply wired that way.

He knew he was gaining on his quarry when his ears
began to pick up noises from the snatch team. Bolan had
no doubt that he was tracking seasoned killers, but they
obviously weren't elite commandos. Green Berets or Navy
SEALs would never have talked to each other as they led a
hostage through the jungle. They would not have let their
gear and weapons rustle through the undergrowth in passing. Silence was the order of the day for true profession-
als, until the killing started.

Which it would, any minute now.

From sound alone, he estimated that the hunters were
about three hundred yards in front of him and still on
course for Braga's camp. Ten minutes later, he had cut their
lead by half, and he could smell his adversaries now—

gun oil and sweat, together with the cheap cologne some foolish member of the team had splashed over himself that morning.

Stupid.

Bolan could have tracked them by that scent alone, but with the rest of it, and all their noise, it was the next best thing to having one of them rigged with a homing beacon.

Bolan slung his Steyr AUG and drew his SIG Sauer P226. The nearly silent pistol had already served him well this morning, and he saw no reason not to use it once again. As soon as he was close enough to start picking the shooters off, he would begin.

Whatever happened next came down to skill, luck—and, perhaps, a dash of fate.

Condor Acampamento

BRAGA'S MEN HAD caught a scorpion and a tarantula, putting the two of them together in a cage made out of chicken wire and betting which one would survive the fight. The spider was not large, by jungle standards, but the scorpion still seemed intimidated by the hairy legs it raised in warning, curved black fangs erect. Bored spectators had started prodding the would-be combatants with twigs, through the wire, when a shout went up from the camp's eastern perimeter.

Joaquim Braga left his air-conditioned quarters, followed closely by Hugo Cardona. Oswaldo Ramos met them near the middle of the camp, a half smile on his face. "Ribeiro's team has found the woman," he announced. "Her husband was not with her."

"So, what happened to him?" Braga asked.

"Sérgio says he left her in the forest."

Braga laughed at that. These "godly" people were hilarious. Molesting children while they forced the natives to wear clothes, collecting money for their missions in the Amazon and spending it on mansions in the States. Such hypocrites and they still called him a criminal for selling drugs to people who desired them. Unbelievable!

"No word yet from the other teams?" he asked, as if Ramos would not have told him instantly.

"Not yet. But Sérgio heard gunfire half an hour before he found the woman."

"He did not investigate?"

A quick head shake came from Ramos. "He believed delivering the prisoner was more important."

Braga agreed. The other squads he had dispatched could take care of themselves—at least in theory. Ribeiro might have lost the woman if he'd deviated from his basic plan, and they would be no better off than when they'd started.

"Very well. Bring her to me." As Ramos left, Braga told the Colombian, "We'll get some answers now. Or have some fun, at least."

Cardona grunted, keeping his opinions to himself, and followed Braga back inside the air-conditioned bungalow. A moment later, Ramos returned with Sérgio Ribeiro and the missionary's wife, the woman rightly looking terrified. If she had known what lay in store for her, Braga imagined she might have lost her mind entirely.

"Sérgio," he said, "you've pleased me well. You are promoted to lieutenant for your work this day."

Ribeiro beamed and bowed his way out of the bungalow, repeating, *"Obrigado, senhor,"* until the door closed behind him. Such a simple thing to make him happy. Keep him loyal.

Braga studied the disheveled woman. Eyes red rimmed from crying. Small cuts on her face and arms, rips and mud smears on her clothing—all apparently from rushing headlong through the forest in a panic.

"Were you lost when my men found you?" he inquired, breaking the ice in English.

"I suppose so," she replied.

"Without your husband?"

"Sim."

"You speak our language?"

"Só um pouco."

"We'll use yours then. Why did your husband leave you in the jungle?"

Now she hesitated, thinking of the answer that would serve her best. At last, she said, "To do his work."

"What work is that?"

"Helping the natives find their way to God."

"While you, his wife, he leaves to die alone. Is that the Christian way?"

"He has a calling," she replied defiantly.

"Ah. *Um fanático*. I know the kind."

"You're wrong. God's calling takes priority over all earthly things."

"I think it was not God who rescued you and killed my soldiers yesterday."

"Can you be sure?"

"Does he use a machine gun?" Braga asked.

"He uses people in accordance with His will."

"And you will tell us who he used on this occasion," Braga said. "Or you will suffer greatly for defying me."

MACK BOLAN STARTED with the last man in the marching column, dropping him with a Parabellum round between the ears, then ducking off to the left side of the trail. When the next soldier in line glanced back, then shouted to the rest, Bolan was ready. Met him with a silent slug that drilled his left eye socket as he came back to investigate the noise his pal had made while dropping dead.

Fear rippled down the whole length of the column, and

someone barked an order from the front. *"Abrir fogo!"* Eighteen surviving shooters opened fire in all directions, automatic rifles ripping up the undergrowth without a clear-cut target, hot brass showering the forest trail.

Bolan stayed low and let the death wind fan the shrubs and ferns above him, dropping tattered bits of camouflage over his prostrate form. He waited till their magazines ran dry, and when the first few started to reload, he made his move.

No hand grenades with Abner in the mix, and he still liked the silent SIG for close-up work, keeping his targets guessing even as they died. He stayed away from double-taps to keep it simple, make the SIG's twenty-round magazine stretch over the duration of the fight, and he moved each time he fired so that his adversaries couldn't get a fix on where he was. It must have felt as if they were surrounded, bullets slashing through their ranks from this and that direction, each one taking down a soldier who'd been standing seconds earlier.

At last, only two men remained. One of Braga's men held a pistol to Abner's head, moving in jerky little circles as he tried to watch all sides at once. "Show yourselves!" he shouted in Portuguese. "If you don't, I'll kill him!"

"Sorry," Bolan told him from the shadows. "I don't understand a word you're saying."

Spinning toward the sound of his reply, the gunman barked, "Come out and show yourself! I kill him otherwise!"

Watching the pistol pressed against Abner's skull, Bolan stepped out onto the narrow trail, his own SIG dangling at his side.

"Where are the others?" his adversary demanded.

"No others. Just me."

"You're lying! Where are they?"

Bolan shrugged. "Maybe behind you. Maybe to your left or right."

"I want to see them all!"

"They see you," Bolan told him. "That's enough."

He didn't understand what the gunman said next, but it didn't sound like a compliment, based on the tone. "You want this one alive, you let us go."

"Not happening."

"And if I kill him?"

"Think about it."

"You kill me, eh? But you still don't have him, if he's dead."

"It's your call, if you'd rather die," Bolan said.

He could see the shooter thinking, almost heard the wheels turning inside his head, considering his narrow range of options. Finally, he said, "You think I'm more afraid of you than of *o chefe?* Stupid *gringo.*"

Bolan saw it coming, dropped into a half crouch as his pistol rose and locked onto its target, half a face exposed just to the right of Abner Cronin's gaping visage, but he couldn't beat the twitch of his opponent's index finger. Muffled slightly by the weapon's muzzle being pressed against his head, the kill shot shattered Cronin's skull and sprayed the foliage to his left with crimson just as Bolan fired.

His shot was dead on target, with the emphasis on *dead.* The man who had been using Abner as a shield a heartbeat earlier slumped backward, dying even as he toppled to the ground. Cronin, released to gravity's embrace, collapsed beside his killer's corpse, a final pose of intimacy for the slayer and the slain.

Cursing, Bolan stripped off the gunman's camo shirt, used it to wrap the missionary's shattered skull, then hoisted Abner in a fireman's carry for the long hike back to Mercy Cronin and the clearing where'd he'd left her, now a widow.

Cold Camp, Mato Grosso

MERCY WASN'T THERE. His time transporting Abner had been wasted, Bolan saw, as he let the body drop. He moved around the clearing, trying to decide how long she had been gone, and finally concluded that she must have followed him that morning—or attempted to.

Stupid!

If she'd been close behind him, Bolan knew he would have noticed her—or would he? Concentrating on the search for Abner, caught up in a skirmish with the first party of hunters, Bolan wondered if Mercy could have been following along unnoticed, far enough behind that he hadn't heard her.

Maybe.

The only other possibility was that she'd run off on her own—trying to find the mission on another course she had chosen at random—and got lost. In either case, she'd graduated from a mere annoyance to an obstacle that might derail his mission, if he let it.

Standing in the forest clearing with a dead man at his feet, Bolan almost decided to dismiss the vanished widow from his mind and press on with his mission. Leave her to the jungle and the elements to meet whatever fate might lie in store for her.

Almost.

But when he thought about it for another moment— more time lost that he couldn't regain—Bolan knew he couldn't face himself tomorrow if he didn't make one final effort to pull Mercy Cronin out of the dilemma she'd created for herself, before it was too late.

One *absolutely* final effort, right, and no mistake. He wasn't in the Amazon to babysit an addlepated dilettante or self-appointed Joan of Arc. One more attempt to help her, and if Bolan could not find her—or if she persisted on a path toward self-destruction—he would let her go.

The only path that led away from camp was the same one he'd followed earlier that morning, on his way to Mercy Mission. Bolan couldn't pick out any footsteps trailing his, but he had no other choice. He couldn't simply pick a random compass point and start his search from there. If Mercy hadn't followed him, though he suspected she had, she was well and truly gone.

As he approached the point where he had jumped the first column of Braga's hunters, Bolan picked out signs of someone else leaving the trail, breaking away from the established line of the march. Had that been Mercy, maybe frightened when the shooting had started?

Once again, he couldn't say for sure, but played the likely odds and followed where the signs led, on a tangent from the trail and off into the forest. Keeping oriented with his compass and the GPS, he hiked another mile and change before the solitary runner's path met that of men marching in numbers, likely yet another team from Joaquim Braga's camp.

And when that column's trail went on no farther, when it doubled back, Bolan knew where he had to go. It might be hopeless, but he had to try.

10

Condor Acampamento

The prefab shed was roughly eight feet wide and five feet deep, its peaked roof maybe seven feet above the flat dirt floor. Its green aluminum walls had no windows, and its only door was padlocked on the outside. Likely guarded too, as far as Mercy Cronin knew.

The good news: she was still alive and hadn't suffered any injury so far. Despite horrendous threats of rape and mutilation offered up with mocking laughter by her captors, she had not been touched so far, except when one of Joaquim Braga's men had clutched her arm and dragged her to the shed that was her prison cell.

The bad news: waiting for the drug lord and his men to carry out their threats was driving her out of her mind.

She wanted Abner, Matthew Cooper—*someone*—to save her from the gruesome, agonizing fate that lay in front of her. The worst part, to her mind, was that she had already given Braga all the information she possessed. No one in law enforcement or from any covert agency had sponsored Mercy Mission to spy against the Braga syndicate. She barely knew Matt Cooper, and while she'd given up his name—a bid to save herself—she couldn't tell her captors who had sent him here. She simply didn't know.

And Braga thought she was lying.

Hence the intermission, while he turned his thoughts to what he called her "special treatment." Based on her "refusal to cooperate," he had decided she must serve as an example to his men and to a visitor whom Braga clearly wanted to impress. She did not recognize the VIP, had not been introduced to him, but she'd noted that he spoke Spanish to Braga, while the common language of the camp—and of Brazil—was Portuguese.

Not a Brazilian then. That didn't narrow down the field much. Braga dealt in drugs, which helped a little. She had read enough about the cocaine scourge to know that most of the big-time cartels were based in Mexico, Colombia, Peru or Bolivia. A Mexican gang would not ship their drugs south to Brazil then back to the States, she imagined. Why double the distance and the risk of discovery, when they could simply cross the border and be done with it?

So, Braga's guest was South American, not Mexican—and what on earth did that matter to Mercy? In a little while, the nameless man would watch her die, perhaps join in the butchery himself. She had no interest in his name or nationality, would never have a chance to finger him for the authorities. Most likely she would die and be forgotten by the outside world.

She had of course considered ways to save herself. Lying might be an option. She could fabricate elaborate conspiracies around herself and Abner, tell Braga that Cooper was working for the CIA, but what would that accomplish? She was not Scheherazade, spinning a thousand tales to keep her own head off a sultan's chopping block. Braga would see through her pretense, would be infuriated by it, and her suffering would be all the worse for it.

Escape? How would she manage that?

There was no fence around the forest camp, but she was trapped inside the shed. If she began to dig bare-handed—tunneling underneath one of the shed's walls—she would still be in the middle of the camp, surrounded by a small army of gunmen.

No. It was ridiculous.

There would be no escape for Mercy unless Braga freed her, and she knew that wouldn't happen. How could he release a person he had kidnapped, knowing that no matter what she promised, she would certainly report him to police as soon as she could reach the nearest town?

Preposterous.

Her only hope, she thought now, was to make Braga so angry that he killed her outright in a fit of rage, rather than through protracted torture. That might be a form of suicide—a sin which Mercy had been taught was unforgivable—but she would rather risk the fires of Hell in theory than face an agonizing death in fact.

WHEN HE'D COVERED half the distance from last night's camp to Joaquim Braga's compound, Bolan knew the timing wouldn't work. Assuming that he did find Braga holding Mercy Cronin, extricating her would likely mean a firefight, which would blow his plan for taking out the Medellín delivery along with Braga and his troops. The flip side—if a miracle allowed him to pull Mercy out and slip away unseen—meant calling Grimaldi for another pickup, then a turnaround to bring him back *again* for Bolan's blitz.

No way.

He was a skillful warrior, and his luck had held so far, but Bolan couldn't change the basic laws of physics. Grimaldi couldn't turn his Huey into a time machine. They had to work within the framework of the day that still remained, or let it go.

And Bolan wasn't letting go of anything.

The clock was running down, same way it always did in any military action, and this wasn't a campaign that could drag on for days, much less weeks or months. He didn't have the luxury of laying siege to Braga's operation, waiting for another shipment if he missed the one coming in this afternoon.

If it came down to one choice or the other, Mercy or the mission, Bolan was a pragmatist. The larger job at hand outweighed one innocent, or two, who crossed harm's path by choice, knowing the risks involved. When Bolan bottom-lined it, he was still a soldier first and not a savior.

But that did not mean he wouldn't try.

And failing, if he *did* fail, he could still make sure that Joaquim Braga never harmed another living soul.

He palmed the sat phone and speed dialed Grimaldi's number, waiting while it rang once, twice, and then his friend answered. "How's it going?"

"Could be better," Bolan told him. "I'm down one, and Braga has the other, the wife. We should go ahead as planned from this point."

On the far end of the line, Grimaldi hesitated for a second then replied, "Okay. I'll get it rolling."

"Same way that we laid it out," Bolan said.

"Roger that. I've got a couple guys on standby at the airport. I can be airborne within the hour, if we don't hit any snags."

That didn't worry Bolan. If Grimaldi said he'd be somewhere at such-and-such a time, he showed.

"They have a chopper at the compound now," Bolan said. "An Mi-24, like you thought from the satellite photos. With the delivery on top of that, it could get crowded in the air."

"No sweat," Grimaldi said. "I'll work it out."

"Okay then. Let me know if you get hung up anywhere."

"I won't," Grimaldi said with perfect confidence.

They cut the link, and Bolan stowed his phone, pushing on along the trail toward Braga's camp. With Grimaldi upstairs to cover him and make sure the load from Medellín had no chance to turn back, Bolan was fairly certain he could finish Braga's operation on the ground. The only question left was whether Mercy Cronin would wind up among the casualties or somehow make it out alive.

Whichever way it went though, Braga's bill was due, and Bolan would collect the tab.

In blood.

Várzea Grande, Mato Grosso

ARMING THE HELICOPTER took about an hour. On his arrival in the area, Grimaldi had hired a couple mechanics who could help and, for twice their normal wage, keep the arrangement to themselves. He might have stretched a point, letting them think he worked for one of the cartels and that his boss would take it personally if they blabbed, but it was his experience that cash and fear in combination held more loyalty than cash alone.

The rocket pods and miniguns were bolted onto each side of the Huey, solidly fixed in place and aiming forward. The pods resembled a cluster of stovepipes, one in the middle, surrounded by six, loaded prior to takeoff. The miniguns fed from long metal belts—known in the trade as ammunition chutes. The guns could be rotated within a designated field of deflection, normally firing twenty-four hundred rounds per minute, but there was built-in compensation for emergencies. When either minigun reached the inboard limit of its arc, it automatically stopped firing, while the other's rate of fire increased to four thousand rounds per minute.

When the whole weapons subsystem was installed, Grimaldi took the pilot's seat and ran his checklist to confirm that everything was operational. His M60 reflex sight was up and running, ammo feed was clear and all sys-

tems were go on the intervalometer control panel. Once
he'd finished paying his crew, and tacking on a bonus he
knew would be appreciated, Grimaldi was ready for takeoff. The bribes he'd spread around air traffic control and
terminal security prevented any last-minute interruptions
before he was airborne.

It felt good to be back in the saddle—or cockpit, whatever. Flying had been his first love, and while everything
about it was enjoyable, Grimaldi found some jobs more
rewarding than others. The best involved working with
Bolan and/or Stony Man. Simple hops from one point to
another, or deliveries to drop zones like the one he'd made
just yesterday, were fine. But for the real kick, he'd take
combat every time.

It wasn't *killing* he enjoyed, per se, although he'd done
more than his share of it. If forced to analyze the rush he
got from live-fire missions, Grimaldi would probably say it
was akin to high-stakes gambling. And, in fact, the stakes
could get no higher than a bet of life or death.

Each time he flew against an enemy, there was the
chance he'd be shot down, or maybe suffer an equipment
failure that would have the same result. Grimaldi had per-
formed a few crash landings in his time, and he'd always
walked away from them. So far. Walking away when you
were under fire, well, that was something else entirely.

And you might not *want* to walk away, if capture meant
a slow death in the hands of brutal enemies.

That's why he never flew unarmed, stacking the deck as
much as possible for his own benefit. If he went down—
and wasn't killed or crippled in the crash—he'd be ready
to defend himself. Or, failing that, to end it cleanly, without giving some sick customer the pleasure of dissecting
him while he was still alive.

Once he was airborne, heading west, Grimaldi pushed
such thoughts out of his mind. He'd never met a pilot who

wasn't optimistic at the point of takeoff. Sure, whatever went up in the sky must later come back down, but pilots— the ones who lasted, anyway—had enough self-confidence to think they would always call the shots on when and where they hurtled back to earth. Only a kamikaze planned on crashing when he got into the cockpit, and since none of them survived, they were an endangered species.

Grimaldi's best friend in the world was waiting for him, counting on him. There might even be a stray civilian in the mix, hoping a winged knight would arrive to carry her away. Grimaldi didn't know if he would have a chance to make her dreams come true, but he'd be there for Bolan, one way or another.

Come hell or high water, the flying cavalry was on its way.

Condor Acampamento

HUGO CARDONA WAS restless. Part of his mind was anxious to be homeward bound, after receiving payment for the cocaine shipment that would soon arrive. He worried about enemies at large, still unidentified, who might pop up and ruin everything. And yet another part was looking forward to the entertainment scheduled for that afternoon.

What was so wrong with that? It was a trait he shared with Roman emperors and other great men throughout history, although open to misinterpretation in the modern day.

A few years ago, a young left-wing reporter based in Bogotá had branded Cardona a sadist, printing graphic details of the punishments inflicted on some of his enemies, particularly traitors from his own cartel. Within a week, the journalist and his fiancée were abducted from a stylish restaurant and treated to an unexpected after-dinner show. For the reporter, it had lasted seven days. His bride-to-be had proved less durable.

Sitting outside of Braga's bungalow and smoking a cigar—one of his Nicaraguan Habano/Maduros, eighteen dollars apiece—Cardona saw the drug lord's second in command approaching. Blowing fragrant smoke in his direction, Cardona asked, "How much longer?"

"Soon, *senhor*," Ramos replied. "The scaffold is nearly completed."

So that was what the little group of Braga's men had been constructing near the center of the compound. It vaguely resembled a child's swing set, built from metal pipes bolted together, chains dangling from the high crossbar with clamps in place of the normal fabric seats. Cardona could not picture how they would attach to human limbs, exactly, but the mental exercise intrigued him.

"And where is your leader?" Cardona asked.

"Questioning those who found the woman," Ramos said. "They heard gunfire before they met her, and the other teams are late returning."

Ramos grimaced as he finished speaking, possibly concerned that he had said too much.

"The loss you suffered yesterday, I take it that's unusual?"

A nod from Ramos. "*Sim, senhor.* We meet bandits sometimes, on our patrols, but they avoid our territory."

"Whereas those who killed your friends seem to be hunting you."

"With all respect, that has not been established."

"No? How else would you explain it then?"

"Perhaps a chance encounter."

"I suppose that might explain the killing," said Cardona. "But the rescue of your prisoners? It's clear the woman must have been released, once she was liberated from your custody."

"We'll soon know all her secrets, I assure you."

"I look forward to the demonstration. Please tell *Señor*

Braga that I wish to speak with him, as soon as it's convenient."

"Certainly, *senhor*."

Ramos was obviously glad to end the conversation and go about his business, frowning to himself. Cardona sensed a certain discontent in that one, which was not unusual among subordinates in his world. There were no altruists in the ranks of organized crime, no selfless givers dedicated to the betterment of others. Every man and woman in a given network was a greedy, grasping opportunist looking out for Number One. Their discontent could spawn betrayal and was something to be monitored, watched closely by the masters whom they envied most.

Cardona knew the risks of power, had eliminated several ambitious underlings who had schemed to exalt themselves over his dead body. Someday, he thought, one of them would be smart and secretive enough to bring him down, but not for some time yet. Meanwhile, he would enjoy his fortune and his freedom to the best of his ability.

His eyes strayed toward the shed where Braga had confined the female prisoner. A guard was posted at the padlocked door, but now Cardona wondered if he ought to speak with someone about getting in to see her privately, before the entertainment started. Watching a performance was one thing. Participating in it personally was a whole other experience.

Braga might agree to let him have a small preliminary taste. Call it a goodwill gesture or whatever. Was it not polite to serve an honored guest before the servants got their share?

The more he sat and thought about it, puffing his cigar, the more Cardona liked the images parading through his head. At last, he rose, stretched slowly, and went off to find his host.

BOLAN CIRCLED ONCE around the compound, saw no sign
of Mercy Cronin and decided that meant nothing in itself.
There were at least a dozen prefab structures where she
could have been confined, invisible to anyone on the perimeter. Meanwhile, a group of Braga's men were building something in the middle of the camp. He guessed it
was a makeshift torture rack, since it appeared to have no
other function.

It figured that was being thrown together for a spec-
tacle.

The warrior's painted face was deadpan, void of all
emotion. If there'd been a nurse around to check his pulse
and blood pressure, both readings would have fallen into
the low-normal range. He was not agitated by the evidence of Braga's plan for Mercy Cronin, or whoever else
the rack might be designed for. Bolan did not get excited,
in the sense of going into battle with a palpitating heart
and sweaty palms.

Somewhere along the line—whether from birth, during
his military basic training or when he had been baptized
by fire in combat—Bolan had been purged of the oppres-
sive worry that debilitated certain soldiers and civilians
dropped into a crisis situation. Bottom line: he had been
living on the razor's edge of life and death for so long
that it was normal for him. Relaxation was the problem,
something that felt almost alien by contrast with his day-
to-day existence.

Things to bear in mind: Grimaldi would be on his way
by now, bringing the hellfire with him. If he suffered no
mechanical calamities along the way, he should arrive
around the same time as the shipment from Colombia,
and at that point, all bets were off. If Bolan planned to
locate Mercy Cronin and remove her from harm's way, it
would be wise to pull that off before the rockets started
flying and the airborne miniguns began to rake the camp.

His problem, then, was evenly divided into two parts—*find* and *fetch*. He narrowed down the list of buildings where a prisoner might be confined, using the process of elimination. Mercy, he felt sure, would not be locked up in the mess hall, in the comm hut that bristled with antennas or inside the shed that obviously housed the compound's generators. Bolan thought she might be in the bungalow he'd pegged as Braga's private quarters and command post, but he was betting on a shed located on the north side of the compound, close to the latrines.

Why else padlock its door *and* place a rifleman outside?

Assuming he was right, the setup posed a series of potentially critical problems. First, he'd be making his move in broad daylight, visible to anybody in the compound. Second, taking out the sentry and the padlock, while not very complicated, would require some time and leave him physically exposed. Third, Mercy might be injured, therefore slowing him down. Finally, he'd have to manage that while under fire from hostiles, while Grimaldi filled the air with slugs and shrapnel, taking down as many Braga soldiers as he could *and* wiping out the cargo sent from Medellín.

All that and executing Joaquim Braga, too.

No problem.

Bolan made his own luck, for the most part, with a mix of preparation, training, personal experience and pure audacity. His enemies were often taken by surprise, believing no one could be dumb enough to take them on. A challenge, in and of itself, could shock someone who'd grown complacent at the pinnacle of power.

Joaquim Braga was in line for such a shock.

And if Mack Bolan had his way, that shock would be the drug lord's last.

11

Hugo Cardona had expected more resistance when he'd asked for time alone with Braga's female prisoner. Perhaps Braga would want the woman for himself. He thought it might be a sticking point, even an opportunity to test Braga's commitment to their budding partnership. However, Braga had simply shrugged, fished in a pocket of his trousers for the padlock key, and said, "You don't have long. The shipment should arrive within the hour."

It had almost been *too* easy, stealing just a little of the satisfaction Cardona had anticipated from coercing Braga into yielding something he valued. Now Braga might believe Cardona owed *him* a favor, or Braga could smirk about his request.

Can't get a woman if she isn't locked up in a shed. He almost heard the cackling laughter as he crossed the compound, feeling Braga's soldiers watching him. They had to know where he was going, what he had in mind. Cardona almost felt embarrassed now, a feeling he had not experienced in many years. It made him angry, and the only person he could take it out on at that moment was the missionary's wife.

So be it.

Braga might have spoiled his moment, but it need not be a total waste.

The sentry standing watch outside the shed stiffened a

little when he saw Cardona coming, though no one would call it standing at attention. If the man were one of his, he would be punished for such disrespect, but that was not an option here. Instead, he simply showed the key and said, "Your boss says you ought to take a break."

The watchman nodded, smirked at him and moved away. Such insolence! It was infuriating. He considered telling Braga of the soldier's behavior, then decided that would only make him sound pathetic. Standing with Braga's key inserted in the padlock, he considered taking out his sat phone, canceling the shipment, but that would have been ridiculous.

The price he was receiving for that cargo quickly changed his mind.

Cardona turned the key, removed the padlock from its hasp and stepped into the shed. It pleased him that the woman cringed away from him in fear, retreating to the farthest corner of her tiny cell. Looking around the place, he saw there was no furniture and that the floor was simply dirt. Cardona scowled at that. Was he supposed to take her on the ground, grinding the filthy soil into his clothes?

Damn it! What was this? Another insult?

He imagined Braga's soldiers pointing, laughing at him, if he came out of the shed with dirt-stained knees and elbows, looking like some kind of barnyard animal. His face flushed hot with anger, focused on the woman who was huddled in her corner, near a bucket that appeared to be the small shed's only furniture. Cardona smelled its contents, thinking she might hurl it at him if he started to approach her.

He would have to kill her then, avenging the indignity— but he would still emerge a filthy, stinking mess, on top of ruining the show Braga had planned to entertain his troops.

Feeling absurd and frustrated, he kept his distance from the woman, speaking in a soft voice as he told her what awaited outside. The chains and hooks, the other tools that Braga had arranged for her. It pleased him when she started weeping, silently at first, then with her shoulders heaving as she sobbed.

This wasn't what he'd come for, but it helped restore a measure of his confidence. He still possessed the power to intimidate, to terrify. Braga should keep that fact in mind before he tried to pull another joke at Cardona's expense. The only men who'd ever laughed at him were dead.

And they had not died laughing.

MACK BOLAN WATCHED the swarthy well-dressed man approach the padlocked hut, say something to the guard that made him leave, then key the lock and slip inside. He wasn't close enough to eavesdrop, but would hear it well enough if Mercy started screaming from the shed—and then what? He was waiting for the cargo chopper, waiting for Grimaldi, waiting for the proper time to make his move.

Waiting.

It was a soldier's hardest job, both mentally and physically demanding. As a Special Forces sniper, he had learned to wait for hours, even days, to frame the perfect shot. Lying immobile while it rained, while insects buzzed and bit, while hostile troops passed by within arm's length, oblivious to death among them. While a vulnerable woman was at the mercy of this stranger.

Bolan wasn't here to save a solitary woman, but to face an army, take them down and send a multimillion-dollar cocaine shipment up in smoke. And yet...

The visitor to Mercy's left just nine minutes after he'd gone in. Bolan examined him, saw nothing that would indicate he'd been in any kind of struggle. He secured the padlock, whistled for the sentry and said something to him as the guard returned that made the lookout's face go slack.

Intimidation games, but that meant nothing to the Executioner. The cargo flight from Medellín was due within the hour. Bolan couldn't watch the sky, thanks to the jungle canopy that loomed above him, but he took for granted that he'd hear the chopper coming. That one and Grimaldi's, too. Bolan would alert Grimaldi via sat phone when the cocaine bird arrived, trusting that his wingman would be nearby and waiting to swoop in when he received the signal. If Grimaldi was somehow stalled or diverted, it would be his job to call, and Bolan would fall back onto plan B.

Same as plan A, in fact, except without the air support. One man against an army, seventy or eighty strong, with nothing but surprise and guts to carry the offensive.

It wouldn't be the first time he had charged the gates of Hell alone.

With any luck, it wouldn't be the last.

JACK GRIMALDI WASN'T stalled, wasn't diverted. He was right on time and roughly halfway to his target, nearly skimming treetop level as he held the Huey around three hundred feet. Rain from a virtually clear sky splashed his chopper's windshield, blowing back in long streaks as Grimaldi cruised along, clocking 125 miles per hour on the whirlybird's airspeed indicator. Birds banked and wheeled out of his path like brightly colored pieces of confetti in a windstorm.

On the vacant copilot's seat to his left, Grimaldi's sat phone lay silent. He hoped it would stay that way, no further setbacks to delay completion of the mission that was swiftly drawing to a close. Another hour, give or take, and he'd be in the thick of it with Bolan, ripping into Joaquim Braga's troops and burning down his house.

Or not.

A last-minute abort was always possible, though Grimaldi couldn't recall Bolan pulling the plug on any operation of this size and scale. Mack was a gung-ho warrior of the old school, dedicated to the proposition that a battle, once begun, must be continued to the bitter end. That meant war to the knife, and knife to the hilt. No quarter, no surrender.

They were up against a good-size paramilitary force this time, on par with Los Zetas or La Línea in Mexico's ongoing drug war. Braga's private army didn't get the same publicity up north, chiefly because its mayhem was thus far confined to Brazil and hadn't invaded the States, but his men were no less deadly than the Mexican practitioners or Colombia's dreaded Black Eagles.

Long odds, skilled enemies. What Bolan had on his side was experience, surprise and a heapin' helping of old-fashioned shock and awe.

And Jack Grimaldi.

The last thing Joaquim Braga would expect, once the battle had been joined, was a literal bolt from the blue. By the time Grimaldi had expended fourteen rockets and thousands of rounds of 7.62 mm NATO ammunition on the drug lord's camp, the last man standing ought to be Mack Bolan.

And if not....

Then Grimaldi would take the message home: mission accomplished, at a cost.

He pushed that image out of his mind and concentrated on the chopper's instrument panel, double-checking altitude and airspeed, manifold pressure for the throttle setting, RPMs on the dual tachometer, compass and GPS. It helped distract him from the image of his old friend lying dead, and it reassured him that he hadn't strayed off course.

When the smoke cleared, and he flew back to Várzea Grande, Grimaldi hoped he would have two reasonably healthy passengers. But he would settle for the one if it was Bolan, having lived to fight another day. That would be victory enough to satisfy Grimaldi.

But he *was* looking forward to seeing the Braga compound in flames.

In fact, he thought, it couldn't happen to a more deserving guy.

THAT COULD HAVE been worse, Mercy thought, then added silently, it *will* get worse.

She had seen her visitor with Joaquim Braga when her kidnappers had delivered her to Braga's camp. He'd taken pleasure in describing what lay in store for her, the tortures she would suffer soon, and while she could not stop herself from weeping, Mercy knew she'd gotten off easy.

For now.

She guessed that her tormentor was one of those people her mother-in-law called a "prevert," perhaps unable to perform with women in the flesh and reduced to terrifying them with words and images of mayhem. Very possibly a sadist, though he had not laid a hand on her, thank God. It was a brief reprieve, perhaps, but it was still better than nothing.

It gave Mercy a bit more time to pray.

She had revised her message to the Lord, stopped asking Him to rescue her. It had begun to sound repetitive and whiny, even selfish, when she knew so many others must be suffering and dying hideously all around the world. Instead, she'd simply started asking Him for strength to bear whatever happened next without abandoning her faith. If she could just hold on to that, until He granted her the sweet release of death…

But Mercy Cronin's faith had taken quite a beating in the past twelve hours or so. It wasn't being kidnapped that dismayed her really, since she'd known her mission to the Amazon was dangerous on many levels. No. It had been

Abner's violation of her trust, his marriage vows that had turned her small world upside down and broke her heart. Wherever he was now, she hoped that he would feel some measure of her loneliness, her pain when it began in earnest, then a flush of guilt enveloped her, making her beg the Lord's forgiveness once again.

It was a vicious cycle, when she thought about it. God supposedly gave humans their free will, then added guilt to make them suffer for it *and* demanded they constantly apologize, on pain of an eternal roasting in the fires of Hell. She thought there was a disconnect in logic somewhere, in the midst of that theology, but even thinking of it felt like blasphemy.

Another sin. Terrific.

Mercy had not eaten since she'd finished off the MRE Matt Cooper had given her before dawn, and now she felt her stomach rumbling, wondered if the guard outside could hear it growling. Braga obviously wouldn't waste good food on someone he planned to kill, so she'd die hungry— which, she supposed, would be the least of it.

What had become of Matthew Cooper?

Mercy had no idea if he'd survived the jungle shootout that had sent her running straight into the arms of her abductors. If he *had,* there was no reason to suppose he could find her, or he would even try.

Unless…

She thought his cryptic mission in the Mato Grosso had something to do with Joaquim Braga. Cooper was clearly not a law enforcement agent in the normal sense; they came with badges and in large numbers, with their warrants, flashing lights and sirens. Nor was he a spy, as she had imagined one, sneaking around and watching people, taking pains not to alarm them.

She supposed he was some kind of soldier. Not a *Chris-*

tian soldier, as the hymn described, but he was clearly marching as to war.

In fact, the battle had been joined.

She drew a certain satisfaction from the thought that after she was dead and gone, Cooper might dispose of Braga and the others. Once again, she felt a pang of guilt—hate was the same as murder in God's eyes—but she defiantly refused to beg forgiveness on that score. All else was taken from her, but she could cling to her rage.

So, how much longer did she have? From what she had heard outside, there was an almost festive mood in the camp. She guessed that Braga and his animals were looking forward to her torture and debasement. Mercy hoped that she would disappoint them, but she knew that she'd be screaming when the time came.

Miserable and alone, she bit her lip and tried to hold the tears at bay.

"TWELVE MINUTES," SAID Nadin Deliz.

Cezar Beltrán glanced at his copilot and nodded. They were right on time, as usual.

Hugo Cardona hated disappointments.

The Sikorsky UH-60 BLACK HAWK helicopter was part of Cardona's air fleet, a U.S. military surplus item he had obtained from the Colombian Air Force. It cruised at 173 miles per hour, over a ferry range of 1,380 miles, and would need fuel after unloading its illegal cargo, before starting back across the border on its way to Medellín. It would be lighter then, of course, after it dropped Cardona's cocaine at its destination.

Beltrán, born and raised in Bogotá himself, had never liked the jungle. All that greenery, with all those animals—hidden until they leapt out at people from the shadows—made him nervous. He was glad to have Francisco Calderón along, manning the BLACK HAWK's M240H machine gun, which was capable of spitting 7.62 mm NATO rounds at a cyclic rate of 750 rounds per minute. He would keep the cargo—and his crew—safe until they landed in Colombia again and all went out for beers, or something stronger.

Flights across the border were innately hazardous, but Beltrán trusted Cardona to make all the necessary arrangements, bribing police and military officers, airport personnel, whatever was required. The money Cardona was making from this shipment, in itself, would keep the average Colombian worker's family fed and clothed for the next thousand years, with money to put all his children through a university, as well.

Beltrán, for his part, made a decent living as a pilot for the drug cartel, a more or less secure position in the present climate, where some six hundred metric tons of cocaine were produced for export each year, despite the various interdiction campaigns and mostly empty threats of extradition to America. He was more likely to be killed by members of a rival syndicate than sent to prison—where, in fact, members of powerful cartels lived like sultans and were often able to purchase early release. Flying an average of once per month with contraband aboard, Beltrán spent thirty hours or so in the air, with takeoff and landing his most vulnerable times. Someday perhaps he would run out of luck. But in the meantime, he was young and reasonably affluent, with the cachet of danger that so many women secretly desired.

"Francisco!" he called back to Calderón. "Be ready with your machine gun when we're making the approach."

"Sí, sí," Francisco answered automatically. He had the M240H machine gun loaded and had test-fired a dozen rounds from its M13 disintegrating-link ammo belt after they were airborne, safely over open countryside southeast of Medellín. The gun worked fine, and Calderón was not afraid to use it.

Five more minutes and Beltrán would radio Cardona to announce that they were homing in, riding the GPS signal provided by the customer to make sure that they did not go astray. The rest should be a simple operation, touching down on open ground, refueling while the buyer's lackeys unloaded the cargo he'd purchased. Cardona would be riding back with Beltrán and the final payoff, possibly relieved to let the jungle fade away behind him like a sweaty, stinking memory.

And they would soon be safe at home once more.

If everything went well.

MACK BOLAN DIDN'T get the radio announcement, but he heard a helicopter coming from a distance. Grimaldi or the Colombians? It sounded slightly louder in his left ear, as he crouched in the shadows south of Braga's compound, so he reckoned it had to be the cocaine shipment closing in. Grimaldi's chopper would be coming from the northeast—Bolan's right ear, more or less—and it was not audible, as yet.

Cutting it close.

If he could hear the helicopter, flying treetop-high at better than one hundred miles per hour, it would soon be visible. Once it had landed, Bolan calculated that unloading its one thousand kilos of prime flake would occupy a squad of ten or fifteen soldiers for the best part of an hour.

Bolan didn't know if riflemen would have to pack the cocaine out to some other location, and he didn't care. His plan was to destroy the shipment here, along with Braga and as many of his men as he could manage with Grimaldi's help.

Or on his own, if it came down to that.

His Steyr AUG permitted launching of rifle grenades,

and one such grenade was already mounted on the Steyr's flash-hider and was ready to fly as soon as Bolan chose a target for its high-explosive charge.

The Steyr let Bolan launch grenades as rapidly as he could mount on the weapon's muzzle and take aim. Aiming from the shoulder meant that he could land explosive or incendiary rounds on target without the bulky addition of a separate grenade launcher under the rifle's barrel.

The *whooping* rotor sounds were louder, closer now. Bolan began to circle north and eastward, toward the open ground where the chopper would touch down, near Braga's Mil Mi-24 Hind helicopter, already on-site. The two together would be sitting ducks for Grimaldi when he started strafing—or for Bolan's own ground-level grenade attack.

No problem there, aside from Braga's soldiers standing ready to defend their lord and master's property. But Bolan also had to think of Mercy Cronin, under lock and key a few yards from the makeshift helipad that would become ground zero when the hellfire action started. Getting in to liberate her would be dicey.

Leaving her behind, to Bolan's way of thinking, was unconscionable.

So, do it all. Why not?

And if he came up short, the world would never know.

12

Hugo Cardona snatched the compact sat phone from his belt the instant it began to vibrate on his hip. Still seething from his frustrating encounter with the female prisoner, he made a conscious effort to control his voice and thumbed the button marked *Habler*.

"How long?" he asked, without preamble.

"Five minutes, *señor*," the cargo chopper's pilot answered.

"Good. Be alert on your approach."

"Is there a problem, boss?"

"No," Cardona said, then hedged. "No problem yet. But be prepared for anything."

"I understand."

Cardona cut the link, hoping his pilot understood, indeed. This was the time of danger for a major shipment, when the buyer had an opportunity to seize the cargo *and* keep half the purchase price. Of course, that would mean war, and he'd seen nothing to suggest that Joaquim Braga might betray him, but it never paid to trust the yes-men absolutely. Knowing that his soldiers would avenge him was no comfort.

How would he celebrate their final victory in Hell?

Relax, he urged himself, but it wasn't so easy. The woman had unnerved him, just as Braga had contributed to his embarrassment, setting a squalid scene for their encounter that would leave Cardona filthy if he had tried to claim his prize. Not a conspiracy, perhaps, but still a joke at his expense, which he would not forget.

A bad beginning to a long-term partnership.

Cardona thought he could hear the BLACK HAWK coming now. Its sound was muffled by the jungle canopy, but it could not be disguised entirely. As it passed, birds scattered and screeching monkeys flung themselves across the treetops in a kind of aerial stampede. Cardona wished he could watch the scene from the air—perhaps on the trip home, where people were more civilized.

Cardona passed the time by calculating figures in his head. One kilo of cocaine, 99-percent pure, sold presently for $3,200. One thousand kilos thus brought him $3.2 million. Braga had paid half up front, meaning that on his homeward flight Cardona would be carrying another $1.6 million in cash. By the time Braga had cut the drugs and packaged them for street sales, he would make a tidy profit on his original investment.

Hugo Cardona was a businessman, perhaps the ultimate venture capitalist, and he did not begrudge Joaquim his massive markup on the cocaine, any more than he complained about the money earned by mafiosi, Cubans, African Americans or Russians who were peddling his merchandise in the United States. Still, it was something to consider, with Brazil being his next-door neighbor.

What if Braga had an accident? Would Oswaldo Ramos be amenable to a revised arrangement? Possibly a partnership that would, in time, allow Cardona to remove Ramos in his turn and rule both countries like an old time feudal lord?

Why not?

The first thing he had learned from Pablo Escobar was that a man took what he wanted in this world. The second thing had been the need to hold what he had taken with an iron fist, crushing any enemies before they had achieved the strength to threaten him.

A gift of wisdom from the master.

Now Cardona was on top, or nearly there. Brazil would make a nice addition to his empire, ruled by fear and generosity in equal measure.

Something to consider, as the BLACK HAWK suddenly appeared above the treetops, like a giant prehistoric dragonfly, and started to descend.

BOLAN SUPPOSED HE could have shot the BLACK HAWK down from where he was, using the Steyr's first grenade, but that was not the plan. He still wanted Grimaldi with him for the final action, and they had some time to spare, allowing for the cargo flight to land, shut down its engines and sit idle while the shipment was unloaded. It would also need refueling for the flight back to Colombia, which looked like it would be another hands-on operation, without benefit of any slick technology.

So he could watch and wait.

As the BLACK HAWK approached, he saw a gunner in the open door behind its cockpit, on the right, manning an M240H general-purpose machine gun. No one else was visible inside the whirlybird, except its two-man flight crew, meaning that Bolan didn't have to sweat a new influx of troops at the eleventh hour. The machine-gunner would be a dangerous opponent, but the mere addition of one automatic weapon to the arsenal that Joaquim Braga had on hand was not a deal-breaker.

Not when one of the Steyr's grenades could take the gunner out, along with the bird he rode in on.

Anytime now. Just as soon as Grimaldi arrived.

Bolan considered Mercy Cronin, wondering when Braga planned to haul her out and start what passed for entertainment in this nest of savages. Would Braga be waiting till Cardona and the cargo chopper left, or would her death be offered up for the amusement of his visitors?

Whichever, Bolan would be points ahead if Braga brought her out himself, better by far than Bolan storming her crude prison hut with Braga's soldiers all around him. Once outside, she would have room to run, Bolan could drop the guards surrounding her—and then what?

Hope their luck held. Hope that none of Braga's people dropped her on the run, that Grimaldi could strafe the camp and not take Mercy down among the hostiles. That she had one more chance to survive, before her life was snuffed out half a world away from home.

That was a lot to wish for in the middle of a shooting gallery—one unarmed lady in the midst of seventy or eighty killers who were panicking themselves, who'd be pleased for any target they could blast to bloody bits. If she could make it to the tree line, if the Executioner could help her, Mercy had a chance. If not, her death would be a quicker, cleaner one than Braga had in mind for her.

Small favors, right, but that was common in the hell grounds, where *no* favors were routine.

Bolan had steeled himself against the possibility of losing Mercy. Not that she was his to lose, by any means, but he had seen lives snatched away from him before, old friends and allies who were now nothing but ghosts haunting his dreams. People no one could have saved, in fact, but he felt the weight of letting them slip through his fingers all the same.

The best he could do for Mercy was to focus on his mission, play it straight. Do everything within his own considerable power to disorient the enemy, wreak havoc on them, raze their jungle hideout to the ground.

The BLACK HAWK settled gently, in a swirl of dust and leaves. Its pilot killed the twin General Electric T700/CT7 turboshaft engines, letting the rotor blades slow and sag as they lost momentum. The doorway gunner stayed behind his weapon, muzzle elevated just enough to keep from being threatening, his eyes invisible behind dark glasses.

Come on, Jack, thought Bolan. Anytime, now.

JOAQUIM BRAGA MADE a mighty effort to conceal his agitation. The scouts he'd dispatched to seek his two missing patrols had returned with more grim news. Another forty of his soldiers had been cut down in the jungle, with no sign that they'd even wounded one of their attackers prior to being killed.

Por amor de Cristo, what was happening? Who was it that had slaughtered more than fifty of his men, and why?

The timing could not have been worse—and, indeed, Braga could not believe it was coincidental. Having ruled out all law enforcement agencies that he could think of, Braga came to rival syndicates. Or was that what the man behind the raids expected him to think?

As he approached Hugo Cardona, standing well back from the circle of the BLACK HAWK's rotor wash, Braga put on his most engaging smile. It would be rash, at this juncture, to give Cardona any hint of the suspicion brewing in Braga's mind. It seemed bizarre to think the Colombian would make a drastic, hostile move against Braga on the very day that he took delivery of his largest ever shipment out of Medellín, but subterfuge and backstabbing was all too common in the murky world both men inhabited. It would have helped to recognize a motive, understand the reason why Cardona would deliver drugs while raiding Braga's ranks, but—

Wait! What if there *were* no drugs aboard the helicopter? What if it were all a ruse to steal Braga's thirty-eight million dollars and change, leaving him empty-handed or worse?

The BLACK HAWK's machine-gunner showed no sign of relaxing as his aircraft settled to earth. He might cut loose at any moment, and while he alone could not anni-hilate all the troops in Braga's compound, other soldiers might be hiding in the helicopter, which, as Braga knew, had room for fourteen men besides its three-man crew. If there was no cocaine on board, if men with automatic weapons suddenly came leaping from the gunship like a flying Trojan horse—

"You see—" Cardona's deep voice cut through Braga's bloody fantasy "—my men are always punctual."

"An admirable quality," Braga allowed, still smiling.

"A necessity for any well-run business," the Colom-bian amended.

"As you say."

"This method of delivery has never failed me," Cardona said. "Once the airstrips for departure and arrival are se-cured, there is no difficulty in the air."

"We hear of interdiction efforts from America. Their President issued a directive declaring that drug traffick-ing by air over Brazil poses 'an extraordinary threat' to national security," Braga said. "Of course, he does not pay our air force. I deal with them directly."

"Good friends in the air force are important, certainly," Cardona said. "I've found them useful for harassing my competitors as well as turning a blind eye to shipments of my own. Imagine the Norte del Valle Cartel's surprise last year, when 60 percent of their crop was sprayed with chemical defoliants."

Cardona laughed at his own joke, with Braga joining in. He hoped the laughter did not sound too forced or artificial. Braga did not wish to spoil Cardona's mood if there was nothing wrong—or to alert him, if Braga's late-blooming worries were correct.

If anything went wrong, he had a pistol tucked inside

the waistband of his khaki trousers, underneath the loose
tail of his floral-patterned shirt. At the first hint of treach-
ery, he was prepared to draw and blow Cardona's brains
out. Nothing that occurred beyond that point would halt
an all-out war.

Hands trembling at his sides, Braga waited to find out
if the BLACK HAWK held a treasure or the end of all his
dreams.

JACK GRIMALDI CHECKED his GPS again and calculated he
was thirteen minutes out from target acquisition at his
present airspeed. He was tempted to reach out for Bolan
on the sat phone, tell him help was on the way, but even if
his friend's receiver had been set to vibrate, it could still
be a dangerous distraction. Bolan would be in the killing
zone by now, planning his moves down to the nth degree
and second-guessing the responses of his enemies to craft
his backup plans, if anything went wrong.

And something always *did* go wrong. That was the nature of a firefight, never neat and tidy like in the action
movies, where the hero never missed, never ran out of ammunition, never took a hit that kept him from rebounding
with a final knock-out punch.

Toss in an air strike, and the chaos increased expo-
nentially.

Grimaldi had been thinking about helicopters. Not
his own so much as Braga's and the cargo chopper from
Colombia. Their satellite photos of Braga's compound
had identified his bird as a Russian Mil Mi-24, once described by Soviet pilots as a flying tank. Its top speed was
208 miles per hour, with a service ceiling of 14,750 feet.
Grimaldi's Huey was slower, with a maximum speed of
135 miles per hour, but he could soar 4,640 feet above the
Hind in a pinch.

Grimaldi's best shot, he decided, was to blitz the Hind

before it roared aloft to meet him in a dogfight. Catch it on the ground and hit it with a mighty mouse, or strafe it first thing with his miniguns and make sure it never flew. That would protect his tail and simultaneously limit Braga's options for escape. Since no highways served the compound, and the nearest river was a mile or more away, grounding the drug lord's whirlybird meant any escape would have to be on foot.

And stranding Braga on the ground with Bolan cut his odds of living through the afternoon dramatically.

MERCY CRONIN DID not recognize the helicopter's sound at first. Two years had passed since her last visit to an airport, and she'd seen no helicopters when she had departed Rio de Janeiro or arrived at her last stop in Várzea Grande. It took a moment for her brain to sort out and identify the noise, helped by the audible response from Braga's men outside the hut where she was caged.

What did the new arrival mean to her? Nothing perhaps. She guessed that Braga's camp must be supplied by air, a luxury he could afford in lieu of having men or mules bring food and other items through the rain forest on foot. For all she knew, Braga might have a fleet of aircraft standing by to serve his every need, from hauling drugs around the world to winging him away on fabulous vacations to some luxury resort.

Why was he living in the middle of the jungle?

Something else she didn't care about.

Her next coherent thought formed as a question: would the helicopter's landing hasten or delay her fate? If it was off-loading supplies, she guessed that Braga's men would be too busy and distracted for the moment to attend her public execution. On the other hand, if Braga had invited other witnesses to watch her being torn apart, she might be running out of time.

I'm running out of time, regardless, she decided, fighting back a fresh cascade of tears.

What could she do about it? Nothing, in regard to breaking out. She'd never picked a padlock in her life and couldn't reach the one outside her door, in any case, even if there had been no guard on duty. There was nothing in the shed that might prove useful as a weapon, other than the slop bucket Braga had left for her sanitary needs. Mercy supposed that she could fling its contents at the men who came to fetch her, maybe swing the stinking bucket like a club, but they would easily disarm her and exact revenge for being soiled.

Ruin their show, she thought. But when her mind turned back toward suicide, she had no means to do the job. Holding her breath was useless, even to the point of passing out, since she would simply start to breathe again once she lost consciousness. If she undressed, her shirt or jeans might possibly be turned into a noose, but there were no convenient hooks or rafters in the shed from which to hang herself. Likewise for bleeding out, since no sharp objects were available.

Mercy had read about a man imprisoned by the Inquisition who had *bitten* through his wrists, the veins and arteries, to kill himself. The mental image sickened her, but Mercy knew it would not hurt as much as being tortured, possibly for hours, while a crowd of savages stood by and cheered through her misery. A little courage, just a bite or two, spit out the salty blood…

Not yet.

She'd given up on praying for release and for a boost in courage, but she had not given up on faith. Not quite. Abner would not be coming to her rescue; obviously she could write him off. But Mercy still held out a slender hope that Matt Cooper might be living. And if so, she knew he would find his way to Braga's camp.

It was the only reason she had ever met him in the first place. He had come for Joaquim Braga and the rest.

And if he couldn't save her, there was still a chance she would be avenged.

MACK BOLAN FINISHED one last circuit of the camp's perimeter while Braga's men began unloading the BLACK HAWK. He watched them carrying the shrink-wrapped kilos of cocaine into a prefab building twice the size of Mercy's prison hut and caught a quick glimpse through its open door, where wooden pallets kept the cargo several inches off the plain dirt floor.

The cocaine wouldn't stay here very long, he realized. Braga needed to cut it and repackage it for retail sales, which likely meant another airlift in the Mi-24 to some other secure location. Cáceres, he supposed, would be the nearest city of appreciable size, boasting its own domestic airport and free access to Mato Grosso's limited network of highways. A cutting plant in Cáceres, or even in the state capital at Cuiabá, would have access to all of Brazil's major markets and others outside the country.

But this load wasn't going anywhere. If it was Bolan's final act on earth, he meant to send it up in smoke.

A quick glance at his watch told him Grimaldi should be arriving anytime now. Since there'd been no call reporting complications, he assumed Grimaldi was on schedule and on course, closing the last few miles before he started raining hellfire onto Braga's home-away-from-home. Whatever happened after that, the coke was history—and Braga, too, if Bolan had his way.

As for Mercy…

Play it as it goes, he thought. The usual.

Bolan scanned the camp for Braga, found him standing with the man who'd briefly entered Mercy's cell before the BLACK HAWK had landed. They were clearly talk-

ing business, each man nodding in his turn; whether negotiating or confirming terms already understood, Bolan
couldn't say, but he did know that none of the authorities
had an undercover operative in Braga's camp. Logging
one more VIP onto his hit list, Bolan used the Steyr's
Swarovski 1.5x telescopic sight to frame the stranger's
face and bring it into close relief.

No recognition there, but he was clearly someone worth
eliminating. Not a problem, since the master plan involved
eradicating everybody in the compound. Failing that, if
any stragglers managed to escape, they could serve Bolan
as his messengers, spreading the word of Joaquim Braga's
downfall far and wide.

A throbbing in the air distracted Bolan from his study
of the stranger's craggy, almost handsome face. He recognized the chopper's sound and smiled. Add this one to
the list of missions where Grimaldi had not let him down.

Bolan imagined the Huey skimming the rain forest canopy, homing on target and loaded for bear. He could picture Jack Grimaldi's face, smiling, ready for anything the
other side might throw at him. Indomitable. Always spoiling for a fight, regardless of the odds.

Bolan knelt in the shadow of a looming giant tree, stead-
ied his AUG, focused on the BLACK HAWK, and started
counting down the doomsday numbers.

Waiting for the sky to fall.

13

Jack Grimaldi's satellite photos of Braga's compound had been fairly detailed, but they'd lacked the close-up quality of skimming in at treetop level, landing struts a few yards higher than the tallest giants of the forest canopy. Suddenly the trees were gone, a clearing some two hundred yards in length and half as wide laid out below.

Ground zero.

There wasn't any signal from the ground, no final order to attack. Bolan and Grimaldi had planned the sequence in advance. Once he had been called to make the air strike, if the raid was not aborted prior to his arrival on the target, Grimaldi was clear to fire at will.

The old joke automatically repeating in his mind was, which one is Will?

They all were.

One quick lap around the clearing, still at treetop level, and faces were turning up to stare at him, two hundred feet and change below Grimaldi's chopper. He could see men scrambling for weapons, some already drawing pistols, and he knew there was no more time to waste looking at the "before" picture of Hell.

The Hind gunship was at the top of Grimaldi's hit list. Circling, he framed the camo-painted chopper with his M60 reflex sight and pressed the trigger for the rocket launcher. His M21 weapons subsytem fired two rockets automatically, one from each side of the aircraft to keep it in balance, their smoke trails converging below as Braga's men saw hellfire coming and sprinted away from its intended target.

Two high-explosive warheads blew on impact, shattering the Mi-24 and instantly engulfing it in flames. The five blades of its main rotor went sailing off in various directions through the compound, cutting down some of Braga's soldiers like scythes slicing through cornstalks, finally hammering into the tree line surrounding the camp. The Hind's three fuel tanks—941 gallons in all—went up next, wafting a mushroom of fire and oily smoke skyward, past Grimaldi's ship, beyond the treetop canopy.

Welcome to Hell.

Ground fire was crackling toward him now, still poorly aimed. His Huey was not armored, although the fuel tanks were self-sealing, but Grimaldi wasn't backing off. Instead, he raked the compound with his miniguns, firing in tandem, watching spurts of sod shoot up as his 7.62 mm NATO rounds hacked their way across the teeming camp. Bodies seemed to explode on impact, the 150-grain full-metal-jacket slugs traveling faster than twenty-eight hundred feet per second before striking flesh and bone. Skulls exploded, arms and legs were severed, torsos gutted by the humming rain of death.

First pass and he saw crimson trails festooned across the camp, painting the grass and soil where green and brown had been the color scheme just seconds earlier. Not everyone who took a hit would die, but the survivors just might *wish* they had, as shock set in behind the initial white blur of agony.

Wondering where Bolan and the woman were, if they were safe, but still far from finished with the little men who scampered for their lives below him, Grimaldi heeled over and swooped for another attack.

As SOON AS Grimaldi's twin rockets struck the Mi-24 gunship and blasted it to scrap, Bolan sent his first rifle grenade hurtling toward the BLACK HAWK. It struck the tail assembly, with its twin Lycoming T55 turboshaft engines detonating with a *bang* that sounded almost muffled by comparison with Grimaldi's two HE warheads.

Still, it did the job.

The ninety-eight-foot cargo chopper carried some thirty-seven-hundred gallons of fuel in its tanks for extended range, and the flash from Bolan's grenade set it off, raising a second epic fireball over Joaquim Braga's compound. From the base of it, a human torch ran screaming, trailing sparks across a stretch of open ground, then vanished into shadows past the tree line on the outskirts of the camp.

Bolan mounted a second grenade onto the Steyr's launcher, raised the AUG to his shoulder and shifted his aim toward the prefab structure where Braga's workers had been stacking the coke they'd unloaded so far. Drifting smoke obscured his view of the target, but Bolan saw enough of it to send the grenade on its way, already up and breaking toward a new position as it punched through the storage shed's thin aluminum wall, then detonated.

This time, smoke from the explosion came out mixed with drifting powder, blanketing a few of Braga's soldiers as they reeled from the impact of the shock wave. Whether it would get them high or simply blind them was a toss-up, but the Executioner was off and running toward a new location, before anyone could track the source of the grenades.

So far, it didn't seem to be a problem. Grimaldi's arrival on the scene, as planned, had all eyes focused skyward while he strafed and rocketed the compound. Bolan used the thunderous distraction to circle westward, moving toward the shed where Mercy Cronin was confined. He'd never have a better chance to spring her from the lockup than right now, while Braga's soldiers focused on a fight to save themselves and their commander.

Firing from the camp was escalating, but the guns were pointed up, trying to drill Grimaldi's Huey as it swooped and circled overhead, blasting the camp with rockets and its brace of miniguns. This pass, strafing from east to west, a burst of 7.62 mm slugs, peppered the trees that shielded Bolan from the open killing zone. He hit the deck, letting the storm pass by, then vaulted to his feet again and put on speed.

He saw his destination through the drifting smoke and thought something was wrong with it, but he couldn't pin it down at first. A few more loping strides and Bolan nailed it down. The shed's door stood wide open, bullet scarred, its hasp and padlock blown away. Its walls were perforated, likely with a burst of FMJ rounds from Grimaldi's chopper on the flyby.

Nothing Bolan could do about it till he reached the shed and peered inside. Bracing himself, he left the tree line, sprinting over open ground.

MERCY CRONIN HAD dropped to the floor of her cell when the first explosion shook its metal walls. Without a window, she could not be sure exactly what was happening, but simple logic told her that the latest helicopter to arrive was firing into Braga's camp. That made her think of Matthew Cooper, the flight he'd been trying to arrange for her and Abner; but she had no time to wonder whether this was all his doing, as the compound popped and crackled with expanding waves of gunfire.

Aiming at the helicopter overhead?

That seemed to be the case, when Mercy heard no bullets rattling past her shed, but she had barely formed that thought when she was proven wrong. There came another roar of aircraft engines overhead, and then a searing stream of slugs ripped through the prefab building that confined her, gashing in its walls and roof, one of them plowing hard-packed dirt within a foot or less of Mercy's face. She lay prone, cringing, until the sudden storm swept past, then dared to raise her head and look around her aerated prison.

Just in time to see the punctured door swing slowly open of its own accord.

It had to be an accident, the padlock being shot away. Mercy could not believe that any pilot would be capable of aiming so precisely—or, in fact, that he would know she had been locked inside the shed.

Impossible. And yet it seemed dumb luck had saved her from captivity.

Not quite, she thought, before hope had a chance to rear its head in earnest. There was still a war raging outside that open door, and whether Mercy left the shed or not, the recent strafing run had shown she could be cut to ribbons, either way.

So why not go for it?

Why not, indeed.

Mercy began to rise, then reconsidered as another thunderous explosion rocked the camp, accompanied by screams and more gunfire. Trembling, she crawled across the dirt floor to the yawning exit, peering cautiously around the doorjamb for a worm's-eye view of the compound outside.

From her position, she saw two helicopters burning. One was larger than the other, with two sets of rotors, one at either end, but neither of the aircraft would be flying any longer. Both were shattered, bright flames leaping from their wreckage, spreading oily smoke throughout the camp. The smaller of the helicopters had the aspect of a broken toy; the larger still retained a semblance of its shape, with its long blades drooping at either end while fire burned around them.

Were there men inside?

Mercy was startled to discover that she didn't care.

She spent a moment watching Braga's men run every which way, panic driven, many stopping here and there to fire their weapons at the sky, when she heard yet another helicopter roaring overhead. Mercy supposed it was the one that had come close to killing her, and fear drove her to wriggle through the open doorway of her recent prison, turning left and starting toward the nearby tree line.

A strong hand clutched her hair and yanked her backward, while a gun was shoved against her cheek.

"Not so fast, *cadela*," growled a man, his voice speaking into her ear. "You don't want to miss the party."

JOAQUIM BRAGA THOUGHT he might lose his mind. Within a few short moments, out of nowhere, a demented madman in a helicopter gunship had transformed his day of triumph into tragedy. The suddenness with which it had transpired amazed Braga, had his brain reeling as he sprinted toward his bungalow to arm himself.

He had a pistol tucked under his belt, of course, as always, but that would not be enough. The rockets that destroyed his army surplus Mi-24 had shown him that he would have to flee on foot if he intended to escape the living hell his compound had become. Whether he'd have the time to rally any of his soldiers was a question still unanswered, but if necessary, Braga thought he could make it on his own.

As long as he was suitably prepared.

In fact he had a bug-out bag prepared for just such an emergency. It contained two days' worth of dried food and bottled water, water purification tablets, a satellite phone, a first-aid kid, a map and compass, matches in a waterproof plastic box, a bush hat and poncho, a survival knife and flashlight, spare ammunition for his sidearm and fifty thousand dollars in crisp American bills. The bag—or pack, rather—was waiting for him in a closet of his bungalow, together with an IMBEL MD-2 carbine with folding stock and a bandolier of spare magazines.

That pack contained all he needed to survive and forge his way through the jungle to Cáceres, where a phone call would have cars and soldiers waiting to receive him. First, however, he would have to flee the compound, maybe take a couple of his soldiers with him, but no more. On second thought, with limited supplies, he might be better off alone.

But what about his guest from Medellín? He had not seen Hugo Cardona since the shooting had started, didn't know if the Colombian was still alive or lying somewhere in the compound, blown to pieces. Nor, just now, did Braga really care. This was a situation where each man was called upon to look out for himself, and devil take the hindmost.

Braga burst into the bungalow and ran directly to the closet where he kept his gear. He donned the bandolier and pack in seconds flat, then checked the MD-2, jacking a 5.56 mm round into its chamber.

Ready.

If he met Cardona on his way out of the camp, by chance, Braga would have a choice to make. Should he attempt to rescue the Colombian and thereby jeopardize himself? Or should he take the necessary steps to rid himself of one more burden?

Wait and see, he thought.

Braga had almost reached the doorway of his bungalow when an explosion rocked the building, hurled its roof askew and slammed him to the floor.

GRIMALDI'S HUEY MADE another swooping run as Bolan cleared the tree line, breaking toward the prison hut. The chopper came in firing rockets and its miniguns, scattering bodies in its wake while Braga's soldiers tried to bring it down with rifle fire. Bolan joined in the deadly ruckus, squeezing off a three-round burst that dropped a shooter who'd run between Bolan and his destination; then he reached the hut and quickly ducked inside.

The place was trashed by strafing from Grimaldi's miniguns, some of the holes in its aluminum walls perfectly round, while others were long narrow slashes. Daylight intruding through the open door helped Bolan scan the dirt around him, seeking bloodstains, but he found none. It appeared Mercy Cronin had survived the near miss, then departed under cover of the gunfire and explosions roaring through the compound.

So where was she now?

Barely five minutes had passed since Grimaldi's arrival on the scene, but fear was a great motivator for speed. If Mercy's luck held, and she'd kept her wits about her, she could have reached the tree line within seconds of leaving the hut and from there...

Damn it!

Bolan had no time to run off in search of her now, even if he had known where to start. He had destroyed Braga's cocaine delivery, and Grimaldi had foiled the drug lord's plan for flying out of Dodge while it went up in flames behind him, but Bolan's mission would not be complete until he stood over the narco-trafficker's dead body.

Simple justice.

Giving up on Mercy Cronin for the moment, Bolan edged back toward the hut's gaping doorway, scanning the slice of Braga's compound it revealed. He crouched in the doorway, waiting for Grimaldi to complete another pass from west to east, clearing the field before him with the

buzz saw of his miniguns. As bodies dropped and rolled—
some limp, some writhing in their death throes—Bolan
broke for cover, headed for the bungalow he'd marked as
Braga's living quarters and command post.

Too late, as a mighty mouse homed in and struck the
prefab building's sloped roof, detonating on impact. The
roof buckled, the walls blew outward, spewing clouds
of smoke and dust. The shock wave took down two of
Braga's nearby soldiers, lacing them with shrapnel as they
fell. Bolan ignored their screams and sought another target,
watching for familiar faces in the chaos that surrounded
him and finding none so far.

No sign of Braga, Oswaldo Ramos or the well-dressed
man he'd pegged as a VIP guest at the compound. There
was still a chance Bolan could find them, dead or alive,
but his next priority was making sure that no one from the
home team called for reinforcements. Angling from the
CP's wreckage toward the comm hut, Bolan began another
sprint for cover, firing short bursts here and there when
some of Braga's soldiers recognized a stranger in their
midst and taking them down.

So many enemies, so little time.

OSWALDO RAMOS HAD considered simply shooting Mercy
Cronin when he'd witnessed her escape attempt, then
flashed on the idea that she might yet be useful to him.
He had no idea which of *o chefe's* countless enemies had
sent the gunship to destroy their forest staging area, but
there was still a chance—a slim one—that a hostage might
aid Ramos in his own escape.

If not, it would require only a second to be rid of her.
A bullet in the head and he could leave her where she fell.

Flying was out. Ramos knew how to fly a helicopter,
even had his pilot's license, but the enemy had wasted no
time wiping out the Mi-24 and the BLACK HAWK from

Medellín. The only other vehicles in camp were two dirt
bikes and one Suzuki all-terrain vehicle, none of which
were truly useful in the jungle without decent trails to follow. Worse yet, they were noisy, would attract attention
when he needed stealth; and none of them was built to accommodate unwilling passengers.

So he'd be walking out with Mrs. Missionary, heading
eastward toward Cáceres. Three or four days, minimum,
of hiking through the rain forest, which meant they would
need supplies.

Still clutching Mercy's hair and hissing threats, he
steered her toward the camp's mess hall. It had been damaged, Ramos saw, marked by a line of bullet holes across
its long front wall. Each one was bright and shiny where
the paint had flaked away on impact, but the metal underneath would start to rust by dawn. The door stood open,
and he shoved Mercy ahead of him, into the dining hall
where several soldiers had concealed themselves.

"Cowards!" Ramos shouted at them. "Get out there and
fight, *pelo amor de Deus!*"

For just a moment, he thought they might turn on him,
but Braga's men had been conditioned to obey whatever
orders they were given. Grudgingly they rose, collected
weapons, then ran out to face their fate in broad daylight.

Ramos shoved Mercy toward the kitchen, at the north
end of the building, grateful that the strafing had not blown
the propane tank that ran the grill and ovens. He released
her long enough to grab a canvas satchel from a shelf below
the serving counter, thrusting it into her hands; then he
clutched her hair again and aimed her toward a rack of
shelves half filled with bottled water.

"Put a dozen of them in the bag," he said. "No! Make
it twenty." Water, Ramos knew, was more important on a
jungle trek than food.

From there, they moved on to the snack food section,

popular with Braga's soldiers, where the shelves were heaped with bagged and shrink-wrapped items such as candy bars and jerky, salted peanuts, pork rinds and potato chips. Most of the items on display were thirst-inducing, but they would not spoil as quickly as fruit or bread in the jungle's steamy heat.

"Go on!" he snapped. "Load up. We don't have any time to waste."

GRIMALDI HAD EIGHT rockets left, and he was circling close to treetop level, seeking likely targets. Roughly half of Braga's prefab buildings were intact so far, and all fair game, but Grimaldi was hesitant to simply take them down at random. Bolan must be somewhere in the camp by now—Grimaldi hadn't taken out the cargo chopper; that had been his old friend's doing—and each rocket Grimaldi fired into the compound was potentially a hit by friendly fire.

Which didn't mean he was supposed to stop.

If Bolan wanted him to back off, Grimaldi would get a sat phone call. Assuming, naturally, that the big guy wasn't hit or rendered unconscious, and that his phone hadn't been damaged in some way.

How to proceed? Stick to plan A.

He nosed the Huey over, framed the largest building he could see in his M60 reflex sight and let another pair of rockets fly. They struck together at the south end of the structure, blew on impact, and he saw the building swell—as if somebody was inflating it—before the roof came off, rising to meet Grimaldi on a ball of oily orange and yellow flames.

Grimaldi banked away and heard something that was either shrapnel or a rifle bullet ping the Huey's tailboom, climbing out of there before it suffered any further damage. Up at treetop level once more, well above the latest flash-fire, he recouped and circled, counted off some thirty seconds in his head, then dived again through roiling smoke.

Muzzle-flashes winked up at Grimaldi as he hurtled toward the enemy, his miniguns humming like chain saws and ripping through flesh much the same. This time the smoke blurred his vision of exploding bodies, but he didn't mind. He took no pleasure from the act of blowing men apart, but neither would it cost him any sleep. The gunmen firing at Grimaldi—then relenting, running for their lives in disarray—had made a choice to be here, to work for a monster and guard his delivery of poison, which was bound for addicts in the cities where those soldiers had been born and raised.

Choices have consequences, all right. Some of them fatal.

And death spared no one in the end.

More *plunk*ing sounds came from underneath the Huey as Grimaldi ran the gauntlet, passing over Braga's camp from north to south this time, plowing a field of flesh. Grimaldi wasn't a religious man, but still he offered up a silent prayer that Mack would keep his head down—and the rest of him, as well—and wouldn't let himself be tacked onto the butcher's bill.

Grimaldi's ammo counter told him that he'd used up roughly half his 7.62 mm NATO rounds so far. How many hits was that? How many more kills by his hurtling rockets? Intel had estimated some two hundred men inhabiting the compound, and Grimaldi still saw plenty on their feet, ducking and dodging as his Huey swept over the slaughter ground. A few more passes then and he would finish off the rockets too, while he was at it. Save a few rounds for the miniguns to cover Bolan when he came aboard, with or without the missionary's wife.

And where in hell was she right now?

14

Mack Bolan reached the comm hut and found its door ajar. Someone inside was shouting to be heard over the sounds of battle, speaking Portuguese.

Bolan couldn't translate, but he got the gist of it. A call for help. It didn't matter to him if the guy inside the hut was calling more of Braga's soldiers to the scene or asking the Brazilian army to jump in. Whoever the lone man was talking to, it had to stop.

Bolan stepped through the doorway, his shadow falling on the young man who was shouting at a handheld microphone, the fingers of his free hand clutching a revolver. He glanced up, saw death before him and let out a squeal before the three-round burst from Bolan's Steyr AUG ripped through the radio operator's chest, ending the call.

No point in taking chances. Bolan blasted each of the devices Braga had arranged along an L-shaped table, taking out a CB radio, a shortwave set, a sat phone setup and a couple computers Bolan assumed were used for anything from Wi-Fi to Skype. He couldn't say who the dead broadcaster had reached, or whether reinforcements would be coming, but at least geography was on Bolan's side.

The closest town of any size, Cáceres, was a hundred-something miles from Braga's camp. Even if the radio transmission had soldiers scrambling now, this very minute, it would likely take an hour or more for them to organize a flight and reach the camp.

Too late for Braga and his friends. Whichever way the battle went, it would be over long before the narco-cavalry arrived.

Leaving the comm hut, Bolan paused again to check the open ground outside, then came out moving like he owned the place, angling toward what passed for the compound's motor pool. There wasn't much to choose from, so he took the Suzuki KingQuad 500Axi all-terrain vehicle, painted in camo to match the rain forest. He found a key in the ignition, waiting for him, gunned it and took off.

Not fleeing. That was far from Bolan's mind. Call it a changeup in the rules of play.

Four-wheeling called for one hand on the throttle, so he'd shoulder-slung the Steyr AUG and drawn his mighty Desert Eagle autoloader as he climbed aboard the ATV. From the first engine snarl it reminded him of an old John Wayne movie, *Hatari!*, about chasing down wild animals in Africa and catching them for zoos.

Except the hunters in the movie took their prey alive.

Not Bolan.

Roaring through the compound on the KingQuad, he kept his right hand on its throttle, the heavy pistol in his left. He started out with eight rounds in the Desert Eagle's magazine and one more in the chamber, quickly burning that one as he came up on a startled runner's right and shot him in the back.

The 225-grain XPB lead-free round struck home with sledgehammer force. The running man was airborne for an instant, arms pinwheeling as he seemed to chase the spray of crimson bursting from his ruptured chest. Before he hit the turf, Bolan was past him on the ATV, chasing down another target.

It wasn't sport, not even close.

Simply another taste of shock and awe.

Hugo Cardona wiped fresh blood from his eyes, smearing the sleeves of his thousand-dollar suit. Something still obscured his vision, and he reached up with a trembling hand to clear it, gasping at the sudden pain. A portion of his scalp was hanging down above his left eye like a cheap toupee dislodged by wind, but this had been no simple accident.

He had been running for the tree line, seeking cover, when a piece of shrapnel from the last rocket's explosion had struck him in the head, a glancing blow that stunned him, knocked him down—and now, as he discovered, nearly scalped him. Grimacing and cursing, the Colombian tried to replace the errant flap of flesh and hair, with no hope of determining whether he had it straight or if it would remain in place. The only good news was that he felt solid bone beneath his fingertips, instead of pulsing gray matter.

His brain was not exposed.

Cardona blundered to his feet, dizzy from his near loss of consciousness and disoriented by his pain, the clouds of drifting smoke, the men who rushed past him in all directions like a mob of specters running willy-nilly through a fog bank.

Where had he been going when he fell? *Away.*

But where? *The forest.*

There was a ringing in his ears, compounded by erratic bursts of gunfire and the *whup-whup* of a helicopter circling overhead. And something else. Was that a motorcycle revving up somewhere behind him, making tracks across the compound? Who could possibly escape on wheels from this death trap surrounded by the jungle?

While he tried to pierce the smoke screen with his bleary-eyed gaze, Cardona reached under his ruined jacked and discovered that he had not lost his pistol. It was a good weapon, a Ruger SR9 chambered in 9 mm Parabellum, but Cardona was not sure he could aim it accurately in his present state, or hold it steady enough to hit a target if he pulled the trigger. Yet better to have a gun than lurch about unarmed when everybody else was firing randomly into the air, into the forest, possibly at one another in the choking, gagging smoke.

Cardona realized, too late, it had been a grave mistake for him to leave Colombia. Whether that error proved to be the death of him was something else, still unresolved. He had survived in other situations when it had seemed there was no hope, but this time…

Trees. He had to reach the forest and conceal himself.

Cardona swiped away more blood—no dangling scalp this time—and saw what he believed to be the tree line, thirty yards or so in front of him. It might as well have been a mile, the way he felt, but he began to walk in that direction, step by dragging step. If he could only make it to the shadows there, he might be able to recuperate.

He might be able to survive.

MERCY HAD NEARLY filled her satchel when a huge explosion blasted through the south end of the camp's mess hall. A ball of flame erupted there, the shock wave hurling chairs and tables toward the kitchen area. Later, she guessed that falling down had saved her, as the kitchen's serving counter took the brunt of the blast and stopped most of the flying furniture from reaching where she lay stunned on the floor. A single chair had banged against her shoulder as it fell, wringing a cry of pain from Mercy's lips, but it had missed her skull and left both of her arms still functional.

She scanned the kitchen space around her for the gunman who had brought her there. She didn't know his name, but had decided he was close to Joaquim Braga from the way they stood and spoke together after she had been delivered to their camp. Some kind of aide or second-in-command, perhaps, as if it mattered now.

Mercy discovered him a few yards from her own place on the kitchen floor, facedown and moaning, bleeding from the nose and lips. It looked as if a coffee urn had tumbled from its shelf and struck him in the face as he was falling, toppled by the recent blast. Perhaps his nose was broken, but his eyes were open, more or less alert, and now focused on her.

"Get up!" he snapped. The pistol in his hand persuaded her.

Rising was not as easy as it should have been. Besides the shock of the explosion and the sharp pain in her shoulder, Mercy struggled with her balance as she tried to stand. Did she have a concussion? Was there bleeding in her brain? If so, she'd likely never know it, since her captor had regained his feet now and was moving toward her, reaching down to grab the satchel she had filled with food and water, thrusting it into her hands.

"We're going," he informed her. "Move!"

She turned to face the doorway through which they had entered, but it was no longer there. Instead, the west wall of the prefab building had collapsed and crumpled inward, forming a kind of chute in place of the door. The gunman grabbed her hair again, twisting it to make her whimper from the added pain, then pushed her toward the gaping exit from the mess hall.

Stumbling, Mercy might have fallen if he had not held her upright. She considered asking him to loosen his grip, but knew it would be pointless. Same for praying, as she reasoned that if God was watching, listening, He would have rescued her by now.

Or sent someone to do it for Him.

She was on her own, it seemed—the next worst thing to being absolutely lost.

THE KINGQUAD'S MOTOR started sputtering on Bolan's second circuit of the compound. Glancing at its fuel gauge, he saw the needle kissing Empty and decided it was time to bail. Instead of switching off the ATV, however, Bolan aimed it at a clutch of Braga's soldiers forty feet in front of him, twisted the throttle for a final burst of speed, then vaulted from the driver's seat to send the squat four-wheeler on its way, unmanned.

Bowling for bad guys.

Braga's men were busy firing at the Huey overhead, deafened by gunfire and the chopper's noise, when Bolan's borrowed ATV slammed into them. It sent two shooters somersaulting through the air and slammed into a third at knee level, taking him down and rolling up onto his back, while others fell away to either side.

Call it a strike, but Bolan wasn't finished with them. He had fed the Desert Eagle a fresh magazine, now emptied it in rapid fire, plugging the KingQuad's gas tank first and sparking flames to sear the gunman trapped beneath it. While he screamed and flailed, the other seven Magnum rounds ripped through his friends, already reeling from the ATV collision with their huddle. When the slide on Bolan's .44 locked open on an empty chamber, he reloaded, then returned the smoking cannon to its holster and unslung his Steyr AUG.

Grimaldi made another swooping pass just then, strafing the ground to Bolan's left. The NATO rounds from the Huey's revolving miniguns came close, but Bolan guessed that Grimaldi had probably observed him firing on the cartel goons, seeing enough at any rate to sort out who was who. The smoke and shifting tide of soldiers wouldn't let Grimaldi track him accurately while pursuing targets of his own, but at least Grimaldi knew Bolan was still alive and kicking ass.

A burst of automatic fire came sizzling in to Bolan's

right, with the distinctive sound of 5.56 mm rounds. He ducked and rolled, eyes closed against the dirt thrown up by flying bullets and the Huey's rotor wash, until he came up in a crouch and faced back toward the source of hostile fire.

One shooter was lining up his IMBEL autorifle for another try, when Bolan hit him with a three-round burst that tipped him over backward, sprawling. Finger on the trigger, Bolan's dying adversary still got off his shots, but they were angled toward the distant treetops, wasted. Whether they'd come down inside the camp or scatter on the canopy was anybody's guess.

How many cartel soldiers left? Bolan couldn't have said and didn't have the time to take a census. Standing still was tantamount to suicide, between the hostile guns and Jack Grimaldi's strafing passes overhead. The secret of survival lay in constant motion, striking hard and fast before Bolan's enemies could orient themselves and take him down.

Still watching out for Mercy Cronin, just in case, Bolan moved on across the killing field, leaving a trail of corpses in his wake.

JOAQUIM BRAGA DID not make it to the tree line. Roaring down upon him from the sky, the helicopter gunship had unleashed a stream of automatic fire, the bullets snapping at his heels until he veered hard right to get out of their way. Too late, in fact, as one slug ripped into his backpack, spalled and pierced his back with jagged fragments.

Braga fell, gasping in pain, but had the sense to lie still, playing dead for a moment, while the Huey passed above him and moved on. He had not dropped his carbine—something of a miracle—but feared to rise and fire after the helicopter as it banked away. First Braga wanted to assess his injuries, determine whether it was even safe for him to move.

And if not...what?

He tensed the muscles of his back and whimpered at the resulting pain. Reaching behind him, twisting awkwardly, he slipped a hand under his pack and found a warm, wet patch that stained his fingers red. He was definitely wounded, but the blood was seeping out, rather than jetting from a severed artery.

Where *were* the major veins and arteries, he wondered, in relation to his spine? He knew of the aorta, but if that was pierced or severed, he should already be dead. Drawing a breath, Braga determined that his lungs had not been punctured. Tensing legs and arms, he found no damage to his spine. The only test remaining was to stand and walk, despite the pain it would cause him. Staying where he was only increased his danger, making death a certainty.

With clenched teeth, Braga struggled up to hands and knees, groaning, then rose into a kneeling posture. Finally, bracing his free hand on his knee, he levered upward, standing, rising slowly to his full height with a final shudder at the lancing pain of shrapnel in his back. It hurt, but he could walk.

Now could he run?

Not very well, he soon discovered, but a loping kind of stride was possible, fighting to keep his balance as new spasms wracked his wounded flesh. The long trek through the jungle to Cáceres suddenly seemed doubly daunting. Could he even hope to make it, or would weakness leave him stranded in the rain forest to die?

Perhaps if he could ride...

Braga turned toward the compound's meager motor pool and saw the ATV was missing. Some *filho da puta* had beaten him to it, but both of the trail bikes were still in their place. Could he manage to drive one, the way he felt? Was it better to try and crash than go off as he was and collapse before walking a mile?

He chose the Kawasaki KLX250S, with its manufacturer's estimate of a 140-mile range on two gallons of fuel in its tank when full. If he could take his time and stay on course—without smashing into a tree or plunging off a cliff—the little bike would carry him most of the way to his intended destination, at a speed unrivaled by a man on foot. Braga could stop to rest whenever he required it, nurse the bike along for safety's sake and still escape the nightmare that surrounded him.

Wincing, he kicked the motorcycle into life and aimed it toward the northeast corner of the camp.

JACK GRIMALDI RECOGNIZED Mack Bolan from the air, despite the smoke and dust of battle, even with the cartel soldiers scampering around him. He was watching as the tall athletic figure sent an ATV slamming into a clutch of Joaquim Braga's men, then started blasting at them with a handgun that could only be a Desert Eagle .44. No doubt about who *that* was, standing in the midst of chaos, taking down the enemy.

Grimaldi banked and circled, coming back to find his old friend on the move once more. Grimaldi chose an angle of attack for his next strafing run that wouldn't threaten Bolan as he kept on mopping up, maybe looking for Braga or the woman who'd gone missing.

Grimaldi still had two rockets remaining, and enough 7.62 mm ammo for another three or four passes across the compound plus cover fire to get the three of them out of here. He had taken hits each time he'd swooped over the camp—one of the slugs starring his cockpit's windshield—but he wasn't backing off. The Huey's fuel tanks, engines and rotors were intact so far, which meant the fight went on.

His targets weren't exactly sitting ducks—not sitting *still*—but even as a few of them slipped off into the rain

forest, more seemed intent on fighting for the open ground
they occupied. That was a bonus for Grimaldi, even when
they ducked behind or into buildings, since the compound's
prefab structures were no match for armor-piercing NATO
rounds, much less his mighty mouse rockets. Instead of
holding back his last two, Grimaldi decided to expend
them on the only structure left of any size.

What was it? He had no idea, but it was coming down.

The Huey shuddered slightly as the rockets exited their
pods to left and right, hurtling away on smoky trails toward impact with their target. Grimaldi kept going, was
above the building when they blew—and something else
went off inside the place a heartbeat later, slamming out a
secondary shock wave greater than the double-rocket blast.

Grimaldi rode it out, his chopper turned into a buck-
ing bronco that leaped skyward on a wave of hot air rising
from the fiery cauldron down below. He guessed it must
have been the compound's arsenal or else some kind of
fuel stash—maybe gasoline and propane stored together
in a dimwit's notion of security.

Flames stroked the Huey's underside but didn't catch,
Grimaldi climbing like his life depended on it. Which, in
point of fact, it did. He used the extra push to supplement
the thrust of his Lycoming engines, gaining altitude faster
than the designers of his airship had anticipated when they
wrote its specs.

Climbing, but just to circle back and dive again into the
smoke and fire. Continuing the battle until Bolan called
him off or he had nothing left to throw at Braga's troops.

Another pass to keep them hopping and to watch them
die.

BOLAN WATCHED THE Huey's rockets strike, then staggered
as the largest fireball yet erupted from the building they
had penetrated. Baking heat enveloped him as he fell

prone, hearing the hiss of shrapnel overhead. Inside that
conflagration, ammunition started cooking off, hundreds
of bullets whining through the camp without a gun barrel
to guide them. Bolan hugged the earth, staying below the
line of fire as best he could, while others bolted from the
fiery wreckage and were cut down in their tracks.

Doing Bolan's job before he got the chance.

Poetic justice, some might say—or just bad luck for
those who took a random hit. Bolan wasn't about to question any break that came his way.

He let the air clear, more or less, then rose and went
back on the hunt. He wanted Braga, Ramos and the well-
dressed visitor he'd shadowed earlier, if he was still available. Taking them down himself was best, but verifying
their demise by sight was good enough. Without eliminating Braga and his second-in-command, the cartel might
survive.

And if he wiped it out, another would arise to take its
place. So, what?

Sufficient unto the day is the evil thereof.

That verse came to him from somewhere in his past,
long forgotten, but it summed up Bolan's take on victory.
There were no final wins in his profession, only constant
battling for the ground gained, then holding on to it and
perhaps advancing a little more.

Two gunmen rushed at Bolan through the battle smoke,
apparently not knowing he was there. They stopped short
at the sight of him, no recognition in their eyes, their weapons rising, but the fight had taken too much out of them
already. Bolan beat them to it, stitched them chest-high
with a string of 5.56 mm tumblers from his AUG and blew
them over backward, shoulders striking turf before their
boots touched down.

The home team, as he saw it now, was thinning out.
Some of Braga's men no doubt had fled into the jungle, but

Bolan couldn't tell if they were watching from the nearby trees or if they'd kept on going, rats abandoning the sinking ship. If they were close, they could start sniping anytime, raising the risk factor, but hunting for them at the moment would be a distracting waste of time. Bolan had to concentrate on targets he could see, the ones that definitely threatened him; no hypotheticals involved.

And here came three more, stalking through the battle haze, two firing automatic rifles at the circling Huey, while the third man clutched a pistol, covering their backs. The lookout had a crazed expression on his face, as if he knew death surrounded him.

Smart guy.

Bolan reached out and touched him with a 5.56 mm NATO round between the eyes, switching his brain off in an instant so he folded like an empty suit of clothes. The others, still intent on bringing down Grimaldi's chopper, didn't notice they'd lost their backup until Bolan hit them with a one-two punch from forty feet and left them sprawled beside the first to drop.

Grimaldi made another strafing run just then, and Bolan tracked him, marking the path of havoc from his miniguns, then following it in search of living prey.

15

Braga cursed bitterly and revved the Kawasaki as the helicopter swooped and made another pass, pursuing him again. *"Desgraçado filho da puta!"* he shouted at the thundering machine, knowing the pilot could not hear him and would only laugh in any case. Behind Braga the Gatling guns began their ripping chain-saw noise once more, spewing projectiles at a rate designed to shred the human form.

He swerved the trail bike, leaning into the erratic veering moves while pain from his still-bleeding back wounds sapped strength from his arms and hands. Braga was frightened that he'd lose control at any moment and crash the bike, perhaps breaking an arm or leg, maybe his neck.

He simply wanted to escape now, would have promised anything to his tormentors, even if he had to lie. Of course, if he survived, he would come looking for revenge; that was a given, but his adversaries didn't need to know that, if Braga could persuade them otherwise. To pull that off, however, he would need a chance to speak.

And at the moment he was fleeing for his life.

A bullet struck the Kawasaki's rear wheel, splintered it and sent red-hot fragments hurtling onward. One pierced Braga's right calf, boring deep, while others struck the four-stroke liquid-cooled engine. Chilled liquid splashed against his wounded leg, accompanied by reeking fumes that told Braga his fuel line had been cut. The bike, already wobbling, kicked free of his grip an instant later, and he found himself airborne.

Braga landed on his back, lying across his backpack and the IMBEL carbine he had slung there when he'd climbed aboard the motorcycle. More pain from his earlier wounds, as the latest impact and his body's weight ground them against his weapon. He tried to roll over, but the crosswise placement of his MD-2 defeated him. Snarling with anger and frustration, Braga strained to reach the nearest quick-release clasp on his rifle's sling, finally managing to get it open as the helicopter circled wide to make another pass.

He rose, using the carbine as a crutch, remembering to brace its butt against the ground and not the muzzle. Standing off balance, racked by pain from head to heels, Braga snapped the carbine's side-folding stock into position and raised it to his shoulder, trying to line up his sights on the circling gunship.

Could he bring it down? Not if he didn't try.

The MD-2 was not terribly heavy—ten pounds with its thirty-round magazine—but it still put a strain on his muscles in Braga's present condition. He fought to hold it steady, aligning the aperture of the rear sight with the hooded post in front, trying to keep his balance as he shuffled through a turn, tracking the helicopter.

When he squeezed the trigger, Braga fired off the whole magazine in one burst, less than three seconds in real time, but he had lost control of the muzzle midway through that burst, could see and feel it climbing as the recoil pulsed against his throbbing shoulder. Stutter-stepping back to avoid the next barrage of bullets from on high, he tripped and fell over again, yet another jarring blow against his spine and punctured flesh.

"Mãe de Cristo!"

Squirming on the ground, he heard and felt the stream of slugs ripping across the turf in his direction, rolling to his left barely in time to save himself.

MACK BOLAN SAW the Kawasaki slide and tumble, but he didn't recognize its driver from a distance, through the battle smoke. One bike remained in Braga's motor pool, not far from where Bolan stood, and Bolan took it out of service with a three-round burst that left the fuel tank streaming gasoline onto the ground. No more escape on wheels for anyone trying to leave the camp. Bolan moved on in search of human targets.

Grimaldi had plowed the camp with miniguns and rockets, leaving wreckage everywhere he struck. The cocaine stash was gone, together with the armory, and Bolan had destroyed the comm hut himself. Too late, perhaps, but they still had some time before any possible reinforcements arrived. Time, hopefully, to locate Joaquim Braga and his chief lieutenant, either dead or living on the field of slaughter.

Bolan started checking corpses as he passed them, crouching to examine faces on the bodies matching Braga's size, if they had any faces left. Bolan had last seen Braga wearing what appeared to be safari garb, tailored to fit him perfectly. There'd been no time for him to change when Grimaldi began to strafe the camp, so bodies dressed in camouflage fatigues received only a passing glance as Bolan moved among them. Oswaldo Ramos had been decked out in a khaki shirt and blue jeans, while the visitor to Mercy's prison hut had been incongruous in an expensive business suit.

Each easy to spot, in theory, but still elusive on the battleground.

And as for Mercy, nothing yet.

Bolan could only hope she'd made it out of camp somehow, when the initial shooting had started. Otherwise, she might be buried under smoking wreckage from Grimaldi's rocket strikes or the detonation of the grounded helicopters he and Jack had blown to smithereens. The fact that he might never find her or discover what had happened to her preyed on Bolan's mind, but he stayed focused on his mission without letting apprehension for the missionary's widow slow him down.

There were enough live targets still in camp to keep him busy, reloading his Steyr AUG, taking them down with single shots whenever possible, conserving ammunition. Grimaldi, Bolan knew, had to be running low on ammo for his miniguns, and once it was exhausted, Grimaldi would be reduced to watching from the air while Bolan finished mopping up.

But there was still time left to find the three specific men he wanted, one of them as yet unidentified but clearly prominent enough to rate a meeting with the Executioner. Three narco-traffickers the world could do without.

Eyes slitted against the acrid smoke, Bolan moved through the carnage, looking for the men he'd come to kill.

MERCY CRONIN CLEARED the mess hall's wreckage, stumbling over slabs of buckled and twisted aluminum siding. Behind her, the man who gripped her hair was cursing steadily in Portuguese, punctuating the obscenities with terse demands for greater speed. Unsteady on his own feet, he apparently could not decide if it was best to shove her forward or to hold her close in front of him, a human

shield. The jerky back-and-forth maneuver made it difficult for Mercy to proceed, but when she tried to tell him
so, he simply twisted on her hair until she squealed.

"Shut up! You draw attention to us, you die first!"

"Aren't these your men?" she asked him, grimacing as
yet another twist sent fiery lancets shooting into her scalp.

"We don't trust anyone today," he answered. "No one!
You understand?"

"Yes!"

"Then move!"

She moved—and immediately slipped on the last bent
panel of aluminum they had to cross before their feet were
back on solid ground. She might have slipped and rolled
away entirely, but the gunman's tight grip on her hair ar-
rested her momentum. Mercy's buttocks hit the metal,
bouncing once, before her captor started cursing her again,
trying to drag her upright.

"Shit! Get up! I said, get—"

In the middle of his tirade, Mercy heard a wet *slap* from
somewhere above her, cutting off her captor's raging flow
of words. The fingers tangled in her hair relaxed, and she
was turning to look up at him when he collapsed. His knees
buckled, striking Mercy across her shoulder blades, and
then he tumbled forward, crushing her beneath his sudden
weight. Warm liquid splashed across her face and neck,
tickling her cleavage as she fell.

The gunman's blood.

He had been shot, and while she couldn't say who'd
done it, Mercy knew the best thing she could do was get
as far away from him as possible. Complete the run into
the jungle she'd begun when he had captured her.

But first she had to wriggle out from under his dead
weight.

Shoving and then rolling him, she managed it after a minute, maybe longer. In the process Mercy felt his pistol gouge her ribs. She relieved him of it, and was on the verge of tossing it away, when something in her mind said, *No!* Mercy held on to it, careful to keep her fingers off the trigger as she finished crawling out from under the weapon's original owner.

He was dead, no question, with a neat hole in his right cheek and a sodden mass at the back of his head where the bullet had blown out a fist-size chunk of his skull. Mercy's gag reflex almost betrayed her, but she overcame it, kept in mind that he would have certainly killed her if it had suited him, without remorse. On hands and knees, clutching the dead man's gun with no clear fix on how to use it, she surveyed the camp once more, seeking the shortest route to cover in the rain forest.

Behind her, frighteningly close, she heard a man's voice. "You should not play with guns."

GRIMALDI CALCULATED THAT he had enough rounds still remaining in his ammo bin to make one final strafing run. He'd save enough to cover Bolan at their pickup, say a couple hundred rounds, but he would use the rest to finish off the nightmare scene he'd sketched over the formerly calm facade of Joaquim Braga's jungle hideaway.

Once more around the battlefield for Bolan and their mission.

Deftly handling the Huey's cyclic stick, collective lever and antitorque pedals, Grimaldi took her down into the valley of fire. Braga's men didn't load their autorifles with tracer rounds, so Grimaldi couldn't spot the bullets arcing up to meet him, but the muzzle-flashes blinking at him from below were proof enough of murderous intent.

Grimaldi couldn't blame them, but he wasn't any man's clay pigeon, either.

This war bird was coming in to kill.

He milked the miniguns for short precision bursts, not hosing down the camp, but spotting pairs and clusters of defenders as Grimaldi swooped to meet their rising fire. It was a hairy ride, but nothing Grimaldi hadn't done before, risking his life for his country and the Executioner.

He watched it all: the bodies jerking, falling as Grimaldi mowed them down; his ship's altimeter; the ammo counter; muzzle-flashes blasting at him from both sides. Banking, as if to come back for another pass, Grimaldi changed the game and hovered where he was, then let the Huey rotate counterclockwise while its miniguns carved out a circle of annihilation in the middle of the compound.

Blood and thunder all around.

He couldn't get them all though, and the ship was taking steady hits. Reluctantly, his ammo counter sitting on a short 225, Grimaldi took the chopper up, ascending vertically to treetop level, then beyond the clearing, for a pass over the forest canopy where bullets couldn't reach him from below.

If he went down again, he would exhaust his ammunition in a fraction of a second, and the odds were even that he'd suffer vital damage to the chopper or himself. That didn't worry Grimaldi so much—he would have done a kamikaze number for the big guy, if required—but Bolan needed Grimaldi alive and airborne at the moment, for the wrap-up of their job.

They also serve who only stand and wait.

Or circle over treetops, as the case may be.

But damn he wished he was down below with Bolan, kicking ass.

JOAQUIM BRAGA COULD not believe his bleary eyes. In front of him, two figures lurched and shambled through the haze of dappled sunlight dimmed by smoke. He stood and gaped at them, blinking, at first believing he'd conjured them from his imagination. Blood loss could produce hallucinations, he was sure, and he'd also struck his head while tumbling off the Kawasaki trail bike. A concussion might have rendered him delusional.

But, no. His eyes and mind were not deceiving him.

Hugo Cardona was approaching with Mrs. Missionary, one hand clamped around her slender arm, the other dangling a pistol. Braga also noted that Cardona had a second sidearm tucked under his belt. He was a two-gun man.

Braga stood ready with his IMBEL carbine as the pair came closer, Cardona wearing a sardonic smile. "You thought to leave without me, eh, *socio?*"

"In my language," Braga answered, "it's *parceiro. Partner.* I supposed that you were dead."

"A grave mistake."

"And you have found the woman. Not that she has any value to me now."

"But she may still be of some use to me," Cardona said.

"We can discuss that when we are secure, away from here."

"Secure, you say? Roaming around the Mato Grosso like tourists?"

"I have people waiting in Cáceres," Braga answered. "It will be a long walk, certainly, but we'll make it. I have packed supplies."

Enough for one, but that would be his secret. All he needed, at the moment, was a chance to raise and aim his weapon.

The Colombian snorted, a sound of rank derision. "I'm

afraid this is the end of our relationship, Joaquim. You are unreliable."

"How do we know this trouble did not follow you from Medellín?"

"Blame me if that's your pleasure," Cardona said. "We are finished, either way."

"So be it. Take the woman and be gone."

"There is one final piece of business to complete, before I go."

Cardona had begun to raise his pistol, but the missionary's wife chose that moment to lurch against him, striking at him with an elbow, struggling to escape. Braga was not about to waste his golden opportunity. He raised the MD-2, aimed hastily and squeezed the trigger, unconcerned with the woman as he sent three 5.56 mm rounds crackling across the thirty feet that separated him from the Colombian. In fact, he'd missed the woman altogether, and it seemed that only one shot had struck Cardona, but it had done the trick, drilling his jaw and dropping him before he had a chance to fire his pistol.

Slumped on hands and knees, the missionary's wife was sobbing, maybe gathering the nerve to break and run, when Braga reached her. Bending down and wincing at the pain it cost, he wedged his carbine's muzzle underneath her chin and forced her head back so that she was facing him.

"It seems you cannot escape me, little dove. Get up now. It is time for us to start our final journey."

OUR FINAL JOURNEY. Mercy Cronin knew what that meant. Wherever the drug lord planned to take her, it would end for her when she was dead. After all that she'd been through—twice kidnapped, threatened with torture and murder, nearly shot just now in a duel between two of her captors—it was enough to make her break down and cry hopelessly.

But the tears didn't come.

Instead, she felt anger's heat warming her face. She stood her ground with fists clenched. To hell with this, she thought. To hell with all of it.

"Go on and shoot," she said. No stammer, no suggestion of a tremor in her voice.

Braga stepped back a pace, the carbine muzzle moving out from under Mercy's chin. He frowned at her, a curious expression on his bloodied face, and asked, "You want to die now?"

Mercy answered through clenched teeth. "Why not? A bullet's better than whatever you'd come up with later. Get it over with."

"Suppose I take you to a city and release you, eh?"

A tiny spark of hope flared, but she smothered it. "No thanks. I'll take my chances here."

"You *have* no chances here," Braga replied.

"You want to shoot me, so do it. Otherwise, you should be running."

"Running, eh? You think I am afraid?"

"From the looks of you, I'd say you were about half dead yourself."

"Far from it," Braga answered. "Maybe I prove it to you now."

"Stick with the gun," she said. "We know that works."

With a snarl, Braga triggered a rifle shot that lifted Mercy's hair on the right side, missing her cheek by half an inch or less. Recoiling from the blast, she dropped to one knee, left arm raised to shield her face, the right flung out to brace herself on the ground—and felt the dead man's pistol shift beneath that hand.

"Last chance," Braga said. "You come with me and live, or stay and die."

Mercy knew the gun she felt was backward, maybe even upside down. She'd have to scramble for it, try to aim before Braga could fire and pray that she could squeeze the trigger. Anything more complicated was beyond her, and she had no time to learn.

"All right, all right," she said, starting to rise, putting a whine into her voice, head down in hopes her dangling hair might help conceal the weapon as she fumbled with it. "If I don't have any choice—"

She came up firing, startled by the pistol's noise and recoil, eyes closing involuntarily. She heard another blast from Braga's rifle, before something hot and wet spattered her face. Gasping, she dropped her gun and raised both hands to touch her face, feeling for wounds.

"You're fine," said a familiar voice.

Matt Cooper. Standing above the corpse of Joaquim Braga, where Cooper must have fired his gun. Mercy saw the gaping wound in Braga's forehead, knowing instantly that he'd been cut down from behind.

"I didn't even scratch him," she said, bitterly.

"You almost got me, though," Cooper replied, as he reached down to help her rise. "You want to ditch this place or what?"

Mercy felt herself smiling, had almost forgotten she knew how.

"I thought you'd never ask," she said.

BOLAN STUCK CLOSE to Mercy as they left the compound, scattered shots still ringing out behind them, but no sounds suggesting organized pursuit. If they met stragglers in the jungle he would deal with them. Meanwhile, he raised

Grimaldi on the sat phone and arranged a pickup on a hilltop they had seen from outer space, through satellite photography, standing a quarter mile due north of Braga's camp.

Make that his *former* camp. The *former* drug lord's final resting place, perhaps.

Bolan had no choice but to break the news while they were hiking, speaking softly both to listen for pursuers and because the news was grim. He sketched the scene of Abner's death, no sugarcoating it, but may have made the missionary sound a little braver than he was. Why not? The tears came then, but Mercy didn't ask to stop. She kept on walking, muttered something that he didn't catch, then lapsed back into silence for a while.

When they had halved their distance to the LZ, she inquired, "What now? For me, I mean?"

"You've still got people from the consulate waiting to see you," Bolan said. "They can review your options, but in light of all that's happened, I'm inclined to say your best move would be going home."

"Home." She pronounced the word as if it had no meaning for her. "Where is that, exactly?"

"Florida, I thought you said."

"What about Abner?"

"I returned him to the site of last night's camp," Bolan said, "thinking you'd be there."

"Of course, I wasn't. Stupid!" Mercy said, clearly referring to herself. "Is there some way we could…get him?"

"Our chopper likely won't have fuel enough to make another detour. Once you get back to the city—"

"Never mind," she said. "He loved this place. More than he loved me, I suppose. More than he loved his own life. Let him stay here."

"No need to decide right now," Bolan said. "When you're sure…"

"I'm sure," she told him. "How much farther?"

"Twenty minutes, give or take, the pace we're going."

"Can we step it up a little?"

Bolan had to smile at that. "Why not."

They found Grimaldi waiting for them, his Huey rotors spinning lazily, not stirring up much breeze at all. He had the Heckler & Koch UMP in his lap, watching the rain forest behind them as they climbed the grassy hill and came on board. He nodded to Bolan, then to Mercy, told them both to buckle up, and in another moment, they were airborne.

Every jungle in the world looks peaceful from the air, a kind of never-never land where iridescent birds and butterflies swarm through the treetops, worshiping the sun. A passerby in flight can't see what lurks below, who lives or dies to keep the food chain operational.

The same is true of cities, more or less, minus exotic creatures on the wing. Bolan had seen both kinds of jungles from the ground, where life and death depended on a combination of intelligence and savagery. He knew the rules of brute survival in the wilderness.

Next time, perhaps, concrete would be beneath his feet. Or maybe sand. Who knew?

Whatever came his way, the Executioner would be prepared.

Epilogue

Congonhas—São Paulo Airport

"How do I know I can trust them?" Mercy Cronin asked, peering through the tinted windshield at a nondescript man and his attractive female companion who stood on the airport tarmac near their Ford EcoSport SUV.

"They're legit," Grimaldi assured her. "U.S. State Department, bona fide."

"Are they deporting me?"

"They can't do that," Bolan replied. "They're from the States. Only Brazilians can deport you from Brazil."

"I bet they'd like to, wouldn't they?" she asked.

"Give them the benefit of the doubt," Bolan suggested. "I suspect they're here to help."

"What if they ask about…you know?"

"They won't. It's need-to-know," Bolan replied.

"I don't know how to thank you," she said. "For everything."

She had thanked him, in fact, more than once, but Bolan let that go. "The best thanks is just getting on with your life."

"Whatever that is."

"Anything you want to make of it," Bolan replied. "It starts right here, today."

Nodding to herself, Mercy got out and closed the Eco-

Sport's rear door behind her, moving toward the consular officials with determined strides. If she looked back, it was already too late. Grimaldi had the SUV in motion well before she reached the couple who'd been sent to shepherd her through reams of diplomatic red tape at the U.S. embassy.

"You've been in touch with Stony Man?" asked Bolan, as they cleared the runway area.

"They're satisfied and then some," Grimaldi replied. "Hal asked me to find out if you need any downtime."

"Something new?"

Grimaldi shrugged. "Isn't there always?"

And there was, of course. In Bolan's world there were no holidays, legal or otherwise. He grabbed some R & R between assignments, when and where he could, but always knew another challenge would be coming up. Another test of strength and cunning against wily human predators.

It was the world he lived in, while it lasted.

And the Executioner was living large, one battle at a time.

* * * * *

Don Pendleton's Mack Bolan

DEATH METAL

Extremists play for hidden nuclear weapons in Scandinavia...

When a Scandinavian heavy-metal band claims to possess the ordnance to wage a war, no one takes them seriously. But then a band member is murdered, and the weapons stash proves authentic. With news of the cache spreading, rabid political and paramilitary groups vie to seize the weaponry. The U.S. has just one good move: send in Mack Bolan. The frigid North is about to be blown off the map unless Bolan can force the warmongers to face the music. And the Executioner's tune is almost always deadly.

Available April wherever books and ebooks are sold.